For Old Friends

Sinkhole Justice

Emerson
"Willie"
Williams

AuthorHouse™
1663 Liberty Drive, Suite 200
Bloomington, IN 47403
www.authorhouse.com
Phone: 1-800-839-8640

All names in this novel are fictitious except for Carr and Melinda Lewis and his brother Clarke and his wife Nancy Lewis. Any words or activities attributed to them in this book are also purely the imagination of the author and probably never took place. Any resemblance to any person living or dead, are also purely co- incidental. Names, characters and events are not to be construed as referring to any living or dead individuals or a reference to any event that may or may not have taken place in the past at or near the geographic points made in this novel. This is a work of fiction set in a real place, Trout, Greenbrier County, West Virginia in the summer of 1865 just after the brothers returned from the Civil War.

First published by AuthorHouse 12/5/2007

ISBN: 978-1-4343-4068-9 (sc)

Printed in the United States of America
Bloomington, Indiana

This book is printed on acid-free paper.

This book is dedicated to my friend:

JOHN R. "JACK" JAMES
10/24/1938 - 02/23/2006

Who really wanted to write a book but ran out of time.

Acknowledgements

I would like to thank my wonderful wife Ann for her patience and understanding and for allowing me the time to express my imagination in print.

I also thank everyone who bought and read "Roaring Creek". The kind words of praise and encouragement I have received are deeply appreciated. I have been told by both friends and strangers that they were normally not readers but they read and liked my book. Many women have told me they were not at all interested in the Civil War but they could not put "Roaring Creek" down until they finished it. Others have said it made them feel as if they were right there when the events in the book were happening. These kind of statements prompted me to continue writing. My hope is that "Sinkhole Justice" is received in the same positive way and provides equal enjoyment to its readers.

The author, Emerson Williams

Holler: Appalachian mountain speech for a hollow, a small piece of land where two or more hills or mountain ranges meet, a small sheltered valley, usually with some type of small stream running through it, but not always.

Sitiation: Appalachian for situation

Sinkhole: a pronounced depression in the land in limestone soil areas, sometimes with an opening for water to drain into the underground streams below the soil level, indicates caves below ground.

Sievey hole: a local name for an opening in the ground that allows water to sink into underground caverns and caves, like a strainer. Pronounced siv-ee with emphasis on e.

Crick: name used for Creek, like Roaring Crick

Lewis Mill, Virginia: became Lewis Mill, West Virginia on June 20th 1863. Twenty years or so after the Civil War it became Trout, West Virginia and remains so today.

Contents

Chapter 1
Thousand Mile Stare

Carr Lewis sat down on the steps of his front porch and gazed out across the fields to the mountains tinted in a light green by the brand new leaves that had just appeared from the jutting branches that had emerged from their winter slumber. He took in the contrast of the darkness of the evergreens against the pale green of the new leaves and tried to wipe the recurring images he had witnessed in four years of war from his mind. The thoughts and tension from the constant danger he had been under for so long seemed to be something he had great difficulty casting away. He knew if he was not careful the images would consume him and he would be like some of the poor wretches he had seen at the military hospital in Staunton. They were sitting and staring toward a far off place and trance like, they would not know or care what was happening to them, in their present surroundings. The soldiers called this the thousand mile stare and said that it could cause immobility that rivaled the loss of one or both legs. He shook his head and with an effort came back to the realization that he was finally home to stay. The war and fighting were over for him and all the others who answered the call to duty for the

Confederate and Union forces in the great conflict that had just been settled with the surrender of the starved Southern forces in Appomattox, Greensboro and all across the south.

He had arrived back at his home in Greenbrier County, Virginia, now West Virginia, (would he ever get used to that change he wondered?) the month before. He had received a minor wound in the arch of his right foot from a pistol shot as his unit the 14th Virginia Cavalry made good its escape from Appomattox Court House. His unit had decided to leave rather than surrender with the rest of Lee's army and the pistol ball was his souvenir from the great war. The ball had been dug out by a surgeon in Staunton and at this time was on his fireplace mantle, a place of honor in his now five year old clapboard farm house. He had built the house just before the war started in 1861 and had spent little time there in the last five years. It was on seventy acres of land just below the top of Twin Sugars Mountain at Lewis Mill, now West Virginia. His neighbor above him, Custus McClung had seen to his place and his brother Clarke Lewis's cabin below him on the banks of Roaring Creek. Thanks to Custus their homes were just like they had left them before the war. He had kept their stock and harvested their crops each year they were gone just like he did his own.

Carr supposed McClung's slaves had done the heavy work of keeping their homesteads going while they were away in the war. Several of the slaves at Twin Sugar plantation had left to join the Union army when they came through and offered them freedom and a 75.00 signing bonus in the last year and a half of the war. Some of the others had left that spring as soon as they heard of the wars end. Many had accepted McClung's offer of a house and wages if they stayed on to keep the place going. There was no real change on the plantation as the crops produced were not the kind to require a lot of manual labor. He grew beef cattle and corn mostly, along with a few sheep and hogs. The biggest crop was field corn and he grew wheat in the winter. The plantation was entirely self sufficient, everything came from right there on the mountain. The furniture was made there and all food grew there in one form or the other. The only thing they imported was cotton for clothing which was spun there and turned into cloth in the early years. In his later days Custus relaxed the self sufficiency attitude enough that he would buy some cloth from a wholesale house in Alderson. This was mind you, cloth only, the sewing and tailoring was done there on the mountain, even his fine suits and silk shirts and scarves were assembled there by his own tailor.

Carr, his brother Clarke and all the other Confederate troops from Greenbrier had returned home to a new state that was run by their enemies of four years, the Yankee sympathizers who had banded together to make a new state of West Virginia loyal to the Union. No where else in America did returning Southern troops face the loss of their statehood except there in the eastern regions of West Virginia. Troops from other states who served the Confederacy came home defeated also but they had failed only at the national level, to form a new nation, they still came back to their same home state. Carr had to come back to the same place only it was now a different state than the one he loved and fought four long years to protect. He was trying desperately to adjust to the new situation but sometimes in the weeks since he had returned he felt like he was trapped behind enemy lines and there was no escape. He remembered reading a book long ago about a man with out a country and he felt that way now down deep inside. The large front porch of his farmhouse though very familiar somehow felt strange and foreign to him. For the first time in his life he felt like an outsider when he had returned from Charleston the week before after surrendering with the rest of his cavalry command to the colonel at the Union fort there. Over three hundred of them turned in their long guns and flags to the victorious Yanks and swore allegiance to the Union. As they made their way back in to Greenbrier by way of Sewell Mountain and Meadow Bluff they talked of the changes that would be coming to their county and wondered aloud how they would be able to control themselves when a victorious Yankee would try to rub their noses in their defeat. They knew it would happen and hoped for self control to be able to walk away with out a fight. They agreed almost to a man that they had endured enough fighting to last a lifetime and wanted only to be left alone in their misery and hoped to rebuild their shattered lives.

They had one thing in their favor though, the people, ex-soldiers and civilians alike of Greenbrier were almost to a man Southern sympathizers. In some of the more western counties of the new state that was not the case. In those counties the returning troops would find themselves very much the minority and suffer more insults and indignities that the Greenbrier troops ever did. In years to come the population of Greenbrier would actually grow because of the influx of ex-Confederates who could not endure the animosity they received from their northern leaning neighbors and moved into the county for a more hospitable atmosphere and friendlier relations.

The local government changed over from pro-southern to pro-northern shortly after the proclamation of statehood was made official. There was no vote they just started the out with the old, in with the new form of government that the Yankee's would run for a few years following the cessation of hostilities.

Carr had attended the wedding of this brother Clarke two weeks after he had returned from the war. He had married a lovely girl from Monroe County named Nancy Williams. The wedding was held outdoors at a lovely waterfall on her parent's farm and was attended by her large family and also some soldier friends of Clarke's. The reception was held at the hotel at Salt Sulphur Springs and everyone had a grand time. Carr had accompanied the bride and groom back to Lewis Mill and had not actually seen them for nearly two weeks now. He decided that he would pay them a visit the next day on his way to the village. The temptation to just stay on the porch and look far off toward the mountains was something he had determined to fight against. He knew that he had to continue on with his life and make whatever adjustments necessary to his thinking and actions to stave off the transfixed melancholy that threatened to engulf him. He must make every effort to get out and see people and become once again a member of his community. He slept fitfully that night and arose early and was back on the front porch again and watched the sun come up in the east. He drank coffee and ate a biscuit with a piece of salty ham for breakfast. He absent mindedly brushed his brown boots and waited for enough time to pass for him to visit the newly weds without having to rouse them from bed.

His chestnut mare Lucy grazed in the field next to the barn along with another mare. Around 8:00 he walked to the barn retrieved his saddle, bridle and pad from the tack room and whistled for Lucy. She raised her head and came up the rise in the field in a relaxed trot, eager but not overly so. She might think we are going back to the war, Carr thought to himself. Lucy had been with him through out the ordeals of the war. She had been his mount on the fields of Gettysburg and all over Maryland and Virginia. He had used her almost exclusively and only changed mounts when it was necessary due to her fatigue and lack of forage. He had been able to rest her for a short time twice, at a secluded farm near Lexington and once near Cass. He had lost contact with her when he had been captured near Lewis Mill in a Union cavalry raid. She had escaped and ran up the holler road all the way to Twin Sugars Plantation and Custus had kept her all that winter. Carr had been surprised to find she was waiting for him when he was exchanged that spring. He had raised her from a filly and she had never let him down no matter how tough the going might get. He saddled up and they made their way down to Clarke's cabin by the creek. He stopped at the fresh grave on the knoll beside that of Clarke's infant daughter, Phoebe, from his previous marriage to Elizabeth a girl from Pennsylvania who could not abide Clarke's enlistment in the Confederate army. She filed for divorce and moved with her family back to the North. He had no idea who was in the other grave.There was no marker of any kind. When they returned from the wedding in Monroe County he had seen it for the first time. Not wanting to disturb the newly weds he had put it out of his mind and not thought on it for the last few days. Maybe, Clarke would know something about it.

He wiped his feet before entering the house where the two brothers had been born and raised. Nancy had the old place shining and clean. He noticed the fresh scent of linseed oil and how the bare wood floors shined. She had obviously been cleaning the inside since she had arrived from Monroe County. The couple seemed relaxed and happy together. She poured him coffee and they all three sat around the worn kitchen table and made small talk. It seemed Clarke had seen the grave too but knew no more than Carr about it.

He decided to go to the store at Lewis Mill with Carr and he kissed his bride goodbye and they left for the village, one riding and one walking, just like they had on their way to enlist in the Confederate army in 1861. Clarke had been in the 22nd Virginia Infantry and seen heavy action in major battles in Greenbrier, the Shenandoah Valley and Cold Harbor near Richmond. He had been captured at Third Winchester and spent six months in Point Lookout Prison in Maryland. He had nearly died from the starvation and ill treatment he had suffered there on that narrow spit of sand between the Chesapeake Bay and the Potomac River.

He had been exchanged on March 16th 1865 just eight weeks ago and was still weak and emaciated from the conditions at the prison camp. He felt the walk would do him good since he had done very little in the way of exercise since coming home to Roaring Creek. They reached the store in about twenty minutes which included a five minute rest for Clarke.

The white store front was elevated with a nice large porch that usually had a few loafers on the bench in front of the window. Carr left Lucy tied to a fence post on the upper side of the store beneath massive oak trees that had provided shade for the store patrons and animals alike for many years. A large hotel was just above the store. It was a large rambling structure and had a water trough out front for the horses and mules that traveled the Cold Knob road over to Richwood and Nicholas County. The hotel did a bustling business before the war and the proprietor was looking forward to a resumption of travelers and customers with the war ending and commerce returning to the region. Luther Brown, the stores owner operated a grist mill that sat on the lot above the store. The water for the mill was provided by a sluice that had been fashioned by limestone rocks. The sluice was filled by water diverted from Roaring Creek by gravity caused by the pitch of the wooden trough inside it and this provided enough force to turn the giant mill stone that ground the meal. The mill did enough business alone to support Mr. Brown's modest lifestyle but coupled with the stores profits the two enterprises were the source of a very profitable business even in these hard times.

Margie Nimrod was the stores manager and she had been there as long as Carr could remember. As a kid he used to think that Margie was mean, but as he grew to an adult he came to realize that what he had taken to be a mean spirit was just impatience with a dawdling boy who could not make up his mind as to which kind of candy he wanted. He had as a boy memorized the contents of the three rows of candy jars. These large jars with the mouth big enough to accommodate Margie's hand and the candy scoop were covered with twist on lids that kept the candy fresh. The first row was horehound, butterscotch, licorice and peppermint. For the life of him he could not now recall the top two rows of jars contents.

There was something comforting about the sound of the floor squeaking as Clarke and Carr entered the store through the front door. The familiar dark wooden counters ran down both sides of the building and across the back. The candy jars were just to the right as they had always been. The shelves above the counters were filled with canned goods. Bolts of cloths, dried meat, the large roll of plain brown wrapping paper and its cutter for wrapping cheese and meat were neatly arranged down the counter top. Across the back counter was the gunsmith section of the store. Shot guns, rifles were in gun shelves built into the back wall and the counters held a few handguns. A familiar sign was tacked to the wall above the shelves. GUNPOWDER AND ALCOHOL DON"T MIX! An inebriated hunter was sprawled on the ground with his shot gun in hand in the picture below it. His head was encircled with spinning symbols showing his obvious light headed state. The middle of the store was taken up with a large Franklin wood and coal stove. It was designed to burn either fuel and was the source of heat for the entire store. Around the stove were a variety of nail kegs that had various kinds of padding added to their tops. Home made pillows covered some of them. Most were covered with simple wooden boxes turned up side down on the kegs. This created a flat surface for sitting and two spittoons were available for the tobacco chewers and smokers. A copy of the GREENBRIER INDEPENDENT, dated three weeks back, served for reading material when the store was empty, as it was now. A sign above the stove read,

IF YOU SPIT ON THE STOVE AT HOME
GO HOME AND SPIT ON THE STOVE

Margie was glad to see the two Lewis brothers she had not seen them since they left for the war, over four years before. She answered their questions about many of the boys of the valley that had gone off to war. Some had not returned and some that had were missing limbs and seemed to have left something of them selves behind when they left the army for home. Clarke told Margie of his new wife Nancy and they talked of a Sunday get together for dinner, but set no definite date. Carr inquired as to Mr. Brown's health and where a bouts. She affectionately said he was as ornery as ever, and was out at the mill grinding some meal. They decided they would go out and see him and went down the wooden steps and across the lot past his one story residence to the red mill beyond it.

Chapter 2

A Prize in Store

Carr had always been close to Mr. Brown who was an 81 yr old bachelor whose only relatives were two nephews who lived near Charleston. He always seemed to Carr to live a lonely life other than through his business. Before the war Carr had worked at the mill part time for Mr. Brown. They had developed almost a father -son relationship and he had stopped the part time work only when he started building his own house and just could not spare the time. Mr. Brown loved running the mill and despite his advanced age showed no signs of considering retirement. His only health issue was that he was an epileptic who had seizures on occasion. He had one that Carr witnessed once and it was not a pretty sight. Mr. Brown told him if he suffered one while Carr was around to place a stick in his mouth crossways to keep him from swallowing his tongue. The seizures only lasted a minute or two and Brown could not remember them when he came around.

They went in the front door of the mill and the first thing they saw was the boots of Mr. Brown protruding from the storage bin toward the back of the building. They raced to the back of the mill and yelled out to him. No answer and no movement greeted them. Poor Mr. Brown had suffered his last seizure and pitched face forward in to the meal bin. He had died when his mouth and nose had buried themselves in to the bin of ground corn meal. He may have been dead before he fell but the way he had dropped face first, had guaranteed his death. Margie was beside her self with shock and grief. Word of the death spread quickly from house to house in the valley and through the hills. People came to the store area and milled about talking quietly among themselves. Mr. Brown had been such a big part of everyone's lives. Most had not realized how much until he was gone.

Nancy rode up in the high wheeled buggy with Custus McClung at the reins. Some one had run to Twin Sugars to tell McClung of the development in the community and he had stopped at the cabin looking for Clarke. Nancy being the take charge kind of person that she was, soon was accompanying poor Margie to her home across the road. She arranged her bed and had the elderly lady resting while the men were getting a wooden coffin prepared for Mr. Brown. A wagon had gone to the shop of Alonzo Wilson who kept a few coffins ready made in his workshop, just for times like this. They sent for the constable a man named Jake Hanson who arrived that afternoon. He spoke with Carr and Clarke, examined the body and signed the death certificate that listed death from natural causes.

Mr. Brown had made his wishes known that he wanted to be buried in the graveyard on Charlie's Knob. This was located northwest of the village on the left side of Roaring Creek. Carr got together a group of men who had volunteered to dig the grave out of respect for the storekeeper and miller. They left immediately to start digging the grave. After a lunch of dried beef, cheese and crackers from the store they began preparing the body for the wake. They dressed Mr. Brown in his best suit, combed his hair and laid him out for viewing in the front parlor of his modest home. People walked by his casket until 9:00 p m: Reverend Rogers the local Baptist minister had been there since the news broke and Carr arranged with him to have the funeral the next day at the Baptist Church south of the store and mill. It was set for 2:00 the next day and was blessed with a bright sunny day. Clarke and Nancy arrived at the church in his farm wagon pulled by Leo the mule. Carr and Lucy were already there waiting. The pall bearers had been selected from the community and they exited the house carrying the coffin down through the village to the small log church. "Amazing Grace, How Sweet the Sound "the hymn selected to open the service began. Reverend Rogers gave a speech about the life of the deceased, about his importance in the community and how much he would be missed. He told of his service to the community and all the good deeds he had performed for his neighbors over the years. He spoke of his attendance and support for the church in his later years. Surely Mr. Brown had a place in heaven set aside just for him and his closest friends.

After the service they accompanied the body up the mountain road to the cemetery set on the hilly cliffs above Roaring Creek. Scripture was read and they committed his body to the earth. The large crowd that gathered to see this good man interred began breaking up in small groups and moving back down the road that dead ended at the cemetery. Carr, Clarke and Nancy went to Margie's house with her. Nancy had brought some food that she had prepared the night before and they ate together and talked more of Mr. Brown and his generosity and how badly he would be missed. Margie said she had something she needed to talk with Carr about and she proceeded to shock every one when she coyly asked. "What are you going to do with the store and mill Carr?

"What ever do you mean?" replied Carr.

"Well, Mr. Brown left his store and mill to you." She said. "I guess you wouldn't know that would you? Since you never had the chance to talk with him after you returned from the war."

She walked to her corner desk in the living room and produced a document that said Last Will and Testament. Mr.

Brown had this made up right after you left for the war. I was to destroy it if you were killed in action. Then, everything would just automatically go to his nephews in Charleston. He said he wanted you to have the store and mill because he knew that you would carry on the business and he wanted some one he could trust to look out for the citizens in this valley. That was very important to him, that the store and mill carry on as before. He said just a few days ago that he heard you were back and if you did not soon come to the village he was going to go up to your farm and see you. He never got the chance to tell you his plans himself. He also gave you $200.00 in cash and the store and mill merchandise that's on hand now. He said that would be enough to get you started. The will was witnessed by my self and Custus McClung. I was appointed executrix and the lawyer Hunter in Lewisburg was to handle the probate on his death. His nephews were not left out of the will. They will inherit a considerable amount of cash plus all of his farm property."

Carr was stunned at her announcement. He had wondered if living by him self in the seclusion of the mountain farmhouse was what he really wanted. The decision about what to do with his life had been taken care of by the kindness of the elderly store owner. He had no training as a store keeper but he knew the workings of the mill. Margie again surprised him with the revelation that she was retiring from the store. Mr. Brown had left her enough, along with the money she had managed to save to take time for her self. She said she had spent over thirty years managing the store and would stay on long enough to train Carr in what he needed to know to keep the mercantile going. She also told him that she had someone in mind to replace her self as manager. Her niece lived in Richland's near Lewisburg and she had experience running a general store. She had been married to a Captain Nelson of the Stone wall Brigade who had been killed at Second Manassas in 1862. The young widow was ready for a change and planned to move in with her Aunt Margie and had agreed to begin working at the store the first of the month. The widow had no children and

Margie was excited about the new arrangement. She of course waited to hear what Carr thought of her new plans.

He said he valued Margie's opinion and would be happy to employ her niece. They decided since it was Wednesday they would leave the store and mill closed until the following Monday. That would give Carr time to go into Lewisburg and see the lawyer. He wanted to waste no time making sure all the legal technicalities were wrapped up before he actually reopened the store for business. Her niece was expected the next morning. She was to ride the stage coach from Lewisburg and should arrive about noon.

Clarke and Nancy had sat by quietly while this stunning news of the will was being discussed. They were surprised to hear of Carr's good fortune and glad for him. Clarke had wondered if his brother was really happy by himself on the mountain. They decided to spend the night with Margie and meet her niece before going back to their cabin.

Carr said he had a lot to think about and left for his farm around four. He and Lucy arrived at the farm just as a storm started and he left her in the barn with two pads of hay and a fresh bucket of water. He high tailed it to the house, getting soaked on the way. The farmhouse was not really cold, just damp and chilly from the pounding rain. He started a fire in the kitchen fireplace and heated some left over coffee. As he drank the coffee, he tried to think of any time that Mr. Brown may have hinted or given any indication of what his plans had been for his store and mill when he was gone. Nothing came to him and the reason for his good fortune was something that he could not exactly put his finger on. Margie had said that Brown wanted someone who would help the community and keep his life's work going. Carr was surprised that he had impressed Mr. Brown as being that someone, in the short time that he worked for him. He would not be one to look a gift horse in the mouth however, If Mr. Brown wanted him to carry on his store and milling business, he would sure give it a try. That reason alone was enough for him to give his best effort toward keeping the business successful.

Carr thought of the time when he, as a kid, had been sent by his father to the store to pick up some gunpowder to be used for the makings of shells for his double barrel shotgun. Carr, as boys will do, dawdled awhile on the trip, stopping to look for trout in the pools of Roaring Creek. By the time he reached the store it was after closing time. He noted the closed sign hanging on the front door and just knew his daddy would skin him alive for returning empty handed ,with out the gun powder, as he planned to hunt turkey early the next morning. Carr could see the door that opened to the back stoop of the store was standing half open. Thinking Mr. Brown might still be back there, he went up the back steps and in to a storeroom at the back of the store. When he stepped inside the door he could hear moans of pleasure coming from the gunsmith area of the store. Margie was bent over the counter with her dress bunched up around her shoulders. Mr. Brown was behind her with his pants dropped around his knees. Carr's face felt red and flushed, he felt like he was about to faint. He must have cried out or made some noise, as Mr. Brown half turned his head and looked over his shoulder at him. Margie's face was turned away from him and she continued to moan and cry out encouragement. Browns' face registered surprise at seeing Carr standing there. Somehow, Carr was able to turn and exit the building without tripping and falling down. His ears rang and the blood rushed to his head in a roar. Margie sprawled across the counter in all her slim nakedness, affected him in a way that was totally strange and foreign to him. The image of her that way would fill his dreams as a teenager. He never knew if Brown told her of his seeing them that way but as an adult realized he probably did not. Mr. Brown never mentioned the incident to Carr and Margie treated him just as before, a dawdling boy who could not decide which candy he wanted. For years Carr could not look at Margie without thinking of her with her dress around her shoulders and always felt his face flush in embarrassment. For her though, it was as if the counter sprawling had never occurred and she of course knew nothing of Carr's later imagination as a teenager. He never told anyone, it had been a secret between himself and Mr. Brown. He knew I could be trusted with a secret, anyway, thought Carr, as he finished his coffee and gazed into the embers of the fireplace.

The next morning Carr was up early and on the road to Lewisburg. He rode Lucy down the mountain road to the village. He stopped at Margie's two story house, she and Nancy insisted on making breakfast for him and Clarke. She soon had a plate of grits, eggs and ham before them in the large dining room off the main hall. She told him to see Hunter the lawyer at his courthouse square office. She said that Hunter had a copy of the will but gave Carr his copy to take with him anyway. He left on Lucy for Lewisburg right after he ate and made good time out the road to Frankford and then on down the Seneca Trail to Lewisburg. He reached town a little after noon and found Hunter at his office. He introduced himself and accepted the lawyer's congratulations on Brown's generosity toward him. All the papers were in order and Hunter assured him he would see that the will was introduced to the probate court. It would probably take about six weeks to get everything accepted and pushed through the courts systems. They discussed Carr taking possession of the store and mill and Hunter said he could see no problem with Carr continuing with the planned Monday reopening of the mill and store.

After his business was finished Carr walked to the City Diner and had a helping of pot roast. As he ate he talked with his distant cousin the owner and told her of his inheriting the store and mill. She said that business was starting to come back after the war. Some of the banks and other business's were being taken over by the carpetbaggers from the North that were moving down here for anything that might have survived the Yankee army. She said she hated serving them and their rudeness made for strained business relations but that was just the way things were now. They were the only ones in town with cash to pay their bill and she had to serve them in order to stay in business. She asked him if the Winslow brothers from Wheeling had been seen in the Sinking Creek valley. He answered that he did not know the Winslow brothers.

She told him they were ruffians who worked for Yankee land speculators and they were trying to purchase land from the ex, Confederates and would take it by any means possible. They had been known to burn barns and houses', she guessed they got a taste for fire during the war. They had burned out a number of poor returning Rebels and stole their farms and land from them. They were a mean bunch who could not be trusted under any circumstances. He said he would keep alert for them and bade her goodbye.

He stopped for a brief rest and drink of water at a spring nestled in a copse of trees beside the road below Frankford. He was sitting on a large rock near the spring and Lucy was grazing at the green grass that grew in abundance near the spring. A group of five riders stopped at the spring. They were a tough looking bunch with a hardness to them that made Carr think of some of the Union cavalrymen he had fought during the war. They were well dressed in clothes that looked brand new and were expertly tailored. Each of them carried side arms that they wore low on their hips like gunfighters and they swaggered when they walked. Seeing him sitting on the rock holding Lucy's reins in his left hand, the one who seemed to be the leader nodded in Carr's direction. He took a long swig of the cold water and looked him over with cold gray eyes. Seeing the CS insignia stamped on Lucy's saddle he addressed Carr as Reb and wanted to know where he was headed. Carr answered that he was headed home and wanted to know why he asked. He said they were the Winslow brothers, land speculators from Wheeling and asked if he owned any land. Not to speak of, Carr lied and said if he did he would not sell it in this economy. One of the others spoke up and said he thought Carr was lying, he bet he owned a nice spread somewhere and was considering selling out. Carr stared at him with out answering. The one who seemed the leader said they would see him again and if he did own property they would buy it one way or the other. They had a way of getting Rebel trash to change their mind about ownership when they finished with them. They mounted and rode slowly away from the spring looking Carr up and down in the most disdainful way. Carr mounted Lucy and rode up to Frankford and turned left out the Williamsburg road.

He thought of the bunch he had just encountered and knew they would be trouble for a lot of people. That kind of new Greenbrier citizen would have to be dealt with by the local people themselves as the courts were now stacked with Union loyalists and if not carpetbaggers themselves they were at the least sympathetic toward them. He considered the situation he was now entering with the store and mill and thought of how just a month ago he was in the army fighting the Yankees. He was really glad the war was over even though it had not turned out the way he had wanted. Sleeping on the ground and being constantly on the move and in the saddle was something he knew he could do without and would not miss at all.

He reached Margie's at seven o'clock that evening. Clarke and Nan were still there along with Margie's niece Melinda. Carr had never seen a more attractive woman. She had large expressive green eyes that sparkled when she smiled. Light brown hair tied up in a loose bun in back and a tall figure with curves in all the right places. She was dressed in a light green dress that accented her eyes and seemed genuinely glad to meet Carr. They talked while they ate supper and he was impressed with her knowledge of store management and seemed to know just what kind of stock he would need there. She and Margie had gone to the store and taken a quick inventory of the stock and she had a few new items in mind that she would like to try there. She was anxious to open the store and get started but was willing to wait until Monday to actually open for business.

Carr found himself whistling to himself as he rode back up the mountain to his homestead. On Monday morning he was at the store at seven a.m. and Margie and Melinda were there shortly after eight. They spent most of the day going through the inventory, checking prices and learning the suppliers that had dealt with Luther. A few shoppers stopped for items, salt, sugar and such. Some of them gave Carr the idea that they were just there out of curiosity and a few were genuinely surprised that he was the new proprietor. Sometimes he almost had to pinch himself at the good luck that had dropped in to his lap. He went out to the mill that afternoon and reacquainted himself with the workings of the business and was glad when a farmer brought ten bushels of corn to be ground in to meal. He liked the way the miller's apron felt as he set to grinding the corn. The familiar smell of the mill and the sound the huge millstone made as it turned was comforting somehow.

He went into the small office and went through the papers Mr. Brown had left of his transactions at the mill. He had kept good records of each days business and had listed the names of every person that owed him money and how much. It seemed he had been accustomed to extending small amounts of credit to certain individuals in the surrounding hills. He had quite a list of bartering accounts where he had taken chickens, a portion of the flour and meal as payment. Even hams and garden items, fruit and other things grown and produced on the small farms were used to obtain items from the store.

That evening he spent some time in the house and took note of the furnishings. He was invited to Margie's for supper and they discussed business over pork chops. Carr was finding himself attracted to Melinda and again was amazed at her knowledge of the stores workings. He asked her if she could come to the mill the next day to look over the accounts with him and advise him on the pricing of his milling services.

As he returned to the house on the mountain about dark he began entertaining the idea of moving in to the house at the mill. It was right at his work and would be most convenient after a hard day's labor. He could move a few of his clothes and things there and if he felt like the ride he could always come to the mountain home any time he wanted. A small field behind the mill could suit Lucy and Carr could turn his farm over to Clarke to work. He would mull this over a few days before he brought up the subject with Clarke and Nancy. He had never questioned them about children but he assumed they would want to start a family and the holler property only had space for a garden. This was big enough to supply them with vegetables but if he really wanted to farm, then Carr's 70 acres would be ideal. It seemed like a good arrangement for all of them, give them a homestead and keep the farm from going back to nature.

The next day Melinda came to the mill and they went over the accounts. He was again impressed with her business sense and she had a way of looking at things with the customer's well being in mind that still showed a reasonable profit. He thought of what a great partner she would make in business and in life. She was so easy to talk to about everything and he found himself telling her things that he had shared with no one, not even Clarke. His hand shook as it brushed hers as they were reached for a piece of paper at the same time. He could feel his cheeks flush and he quickly looked away. She seemed not to notice but he could tell that she was aware of his interest. He felt that he should not rush things with this wonderful, beautiful woman and forced himself to pay attention to what she was saying and not just the warm pleasing lilt of her voice. They talked for three hours and he learned some basic principles of bookkeeping from her and something else as well. He learned that he had to have this woman as his own and would spend the rest of his life with her. After she went back to the store, he sat and thought about nothing but her for an hour. He had little experience with women but he knew this had to be love he was feeling for this lovely green-eyed creature. He decided that he would talk to Margie about this situation. She would know what he should do next. He was shaken from his daydream by the howl of some kind of animal coming from out side the front door of the mill.

Chapter 3

Surprise Stop Over

Morgan Eggleston was on the way home from the war. He had ceased caring who would win months ago. He had walked off from his unit after the battle at Fishers Hill in the Shenandoah Valley. They had held their own for a good while, actually whipped the Yankees and ran them back down the valley toward Winchester. Then Sheridan came riding up on his black charger and rallied the blue troops to turn around and make a run at the celebrating gray soldiers. Since they had five to every one of the Reb troops it quickly became a rout and this time the Confederates were the ones running. Morgan just decided all of a sudden that he had had a belly full of fighting and just didn't give a shit any more. As the rest of the Confederate troops went south toward Waynesboro, he went down a side road to the west and within a few minutes the sounds of the army were in the distance. He spent the first night in a barn burrowing down in the hay like a mole. He had been in the army for over two years now and did not see any chance of things getting better for him. He thought of his shack in the mountains and his wife Maggie who he couldn't say he loved but she was warm on cold winter nights and was not against doing the deed with him from time to time.

The next night he caught a chicken and roasted it on a fire in the pines and ate his fill, even saving the legs for later. He fell off to sleep and awoke to the sounds of horses galloping and men shouting as they came through the pines toward him. He lit out around the hill as fast as he could run and they still seemed to be gaining on him. His lungs felt like fire in his chest and his side ached as he sucked air in great gulps. He threw down his rifle and seemed to get a second wind as his legs seemed to push his feet forward in great driving strides. He heard something behind him, gaining on him, even as he sprinted wide open like he never had before. The noise sounded like a wild animal, with deep guttural snarls emanating from behind him. Something slammed in to his back and he went sprawling end over end down the side of the steep bank. He tried to gain his feet again as the growling bundle of hair hurled itself down the hill and again knocked him off his feet. He rolled in to the side of a giant rotted log with the center missing. Trying to cover his face and throat he hurled himself in to the rotted opening. His face and head went into the opening up to his shoulders as the gnashing teeth tore into his legs and feet. The power of the things jaws was unbelievable as they clamped in to his calves and shins. He could feel the flesh being torn from the bones. He kicked and screamed insanely and his screams seemed magnified to him inside the log. The pressure from the jaws lessened while waves of burning pain cascaded up his thighs in waves.

He felt hands on each of his ankles and he was pulled out of the tree and hurled to the side like a rag doll. Morgan looked up to see the face of the wolf-dog snarling at him with his own blood dripping from its fangs and jaws. It was being held back by a giant of a man with one huge orange eye staring right at Morgan and a socket with skin grown over it where the other eye should be. When he jerked the thick leather collar the wolf=dog tried to turn its head and bite him.

"Down Wolf"

"Down Wolf. He wants more blood," snickered the giant.

Morgan was thrown over the back of a horse and bounced and puked his chicken all the way to the mountain village where he was thrown in to the lean to jail dug in to the hillside. An elderly doctor came to the jail the next morning and bandaged his ribbon cut lower legs and gave him some laudanum for the pain. Morgan slept for days and dreamed of beaches of white sand and clear blue water.

The giant was a sergeant in the Virginia Home Guards. His job was to pick up stragglers and deserters and return them to the army where they were either shot as an example, or flogged and branded with a D on their cheek. He loved his job and was paid a bounty for each prisoner he brought back to the army. He had been chasing escaped slaves to supplement his income and the wolf-dog that he called just Wolf was as mean as the sergeant. He never failed to catch his prey and Sharlot the sergeant had to be sure not to let him loose until the prey was very close or he would kill or maim the prisoner before he could get to him and pull him off the terrified prey. This was of particular importance when they were chasing slaves as the owners did not want to pay for mutilated property.

Morgan suffered in the confinement all winter long and he was fed just enough to keep him alive. Sharlot did not want to take him in until he healed and could walk. He was afraid the authorities would chastise him for having the vicious dog. A strange thing happened that winter, Wolf was put in the cell next to Morgan and over the course of time seemed to grow to accept him as being part of the daily routine. Morgan would have nightmares about the incidence in the pines and wake up to see the dog looking at him through the bars. He would share his food with him some time as Sharlot would remove his muzzle while he was in the cell.

Morgan would repeatedly ask when he would be let out, it got to a point that he would have taken his chances with the army if it would have got him out of that shithouse of a jail. His legs had healed by March, the skin had finally grown over the wounds and his lower legs looked like the wide wales of corduroy pants. Sharlot said that the army had left the valley and he would not go all the way to Richmond for the bounty of just one prisoner. He said he would need to catch more deserters to make it worthwhile. He could make lots more running down slaves than homesick deserters. Nearly every night he would take Wolf and his ruffian friends and work the back roads for runaways.

In early April he brought in some deserters from an artillery company who told Morgan that the war was about over. They said that Lee's army was out of the trenches at Petersburg and was on their way west. The siege was over and Lee's army was being chased by Grant's army with Sheridan's cavalry pressing them every day.

Sometime in early May, about the tenth Morgan figured, they woke up to the fact that their cells were not locked. During the night while they slept they had been unlocked by Sharlot or one of his flunkies. Unbelieving, Morgan could see that the hasp on his padlock was slightly open, when he jiggled the chain the bars swung open. He and the other three soldiers walked to the front and out the door. The street was deserted except for an older lady who was sweeping the floor of her front porch across the dirt road that served as a street. Morgan approached her and asked where everyone at the jail was, not mentioning that he was a prisoner there.

"They have gone," she answered.

"Gone? Gone where?"

"Gone home, the war is over. They don't need no military jail now, there ain't no military. They all left last night. General Lee surrendered his army last month." she said, "Where have you been asleep? That's almost old news now."

The other prisoners were going south and they left right away. Morgan thought of Wolf, he was still locked in the cell. He could not bring himself to leave the animal locked up to starve and he knew that he could not let him loose in the town. He would have to take him with him for a ways at least. He went inside the jail and Wolf was staring at him through the bars. Morgan found some cornbread in the cupboard near a cook stove and ate some hurriedly. He washed it down with some tepid water in the water bucket. He poured some water in a dirty bowl that was just inside the dog's cell, he gulped it down. Then he carefully tossed the cornbread through the wooden bars and watched the wolf-dog gulp it down. Here goes, he said as he opened the cell with the heavy muzzle in his hand. Wolf made no move only looked at him with the yellow eyes. He slid the muzzle over his head and around the fangs, next, he attached a heavy rope to the collar around his neck. He sighed in relief that he still had all his fingers and lead the wolf out the door and down the street toward the west.

They walked west for two days and then headed south toward Greenbrier. Any doubt Morgan may have had about the wolf being dangerous was dispelled when he had to pull him back from three different people who for some reason made the wolf lung toward them with the muzzle on his face. Morgan was able to beg from strangers enough food to keep them alive. He told inquirers of the wolf's disposition, that he was his handler and the dog was specially trained to protect Jefferson Davis and his family and had lived the war at the Confederate White House. This falsehood would sometimes earn them a piece of bacon or an occasional biscuit.

They had been plodding along for nearly two weeks when they rounded a turn in the road and there stood a mule at the side of the road. He, unlike every horse and mule they had encountered, seemed to pay no attention at all to Wolf, Every other animal on the trip had steered clear of the wolf-dog and watched him warily with wide eyes. This one stood and let Morgan pat his nose. He led him to a stump near the roadbed and settled on his back and used the rope on his head to guide him on up the road. He was willing to take the chance that his owner was nearby in order to get some transportation and give his aching feet a rest. Wolf trotted along beside Morgan and the mule and they came up the valley to Lewis Mill three days later.

As they rounded the bend and approached the general store, Miss Margie Nimrod was on the front porch with a rag washing the big window above the bench. She returned Morgan's greeting with out recognizing him at first and then was genuinely glad to see him. He told her he was home from the war and anxious to see his wife and home. She offered him some cheese and crackers and he tied up the mule and wrapped the rope that was holding the wolf securely around his hand. He sat on the bench and ate while she told him about Luther Brown dying and leaving the store and mill to Carr. She told him Carr was at the mill and he insisted on saying hello to him. He removed the muzzle from the wolf and fed him a cracker as they walked to the mill. When they got almost to the front door of the mill Wolf stopped and raised his head and let out the long howl that can make the hair stand up on your back from a distance and scare you to death up close. Carr heard the howl coming from right outside the front door of the mill and opened the door in a run. As he did Wolf broke off the wail and lunged right for him. Morgan jerked back as Wolf jerked forward and he was cut short of reaching Carr. The snarling face and snapping teeth were within an inch of Carr's face with the wolf standing upright on its hind legs. Morgan pulled the wolf down and held him until the snarling abated and then slipped the muzzle down over his dripping fangs.

Carr felt his heart pounding in his chest, the suddenness of the attack left him stunned.

"Morgan, what kind of animal is that?" he croaked, when he recognized the raggedy gray soldier trying to hold back the snarling wolf.

"He's mostly wolf, with a mix of some kind of sheepdog and must have some gunpowder in him too because he's ready to explode at any time. I sure am sorry Carr." He apologized for the attack and went on to explain why he had the animal and told of his adventures of the last few months, leaving out his desertion. But, Carr had a pretty good idea he had been in the jail for that reason. Carr told him of inheriting the store and mill. He asked him when he had eaten last and Morgan told him of the cheese and crackers he had eaten on the store porch. Morgan seemed anxious to get to his home and rest and

Carr could relate to that as he remembered his own return the month before. They discussed the danger of having an attack animal like Wolf around and Morgan said he intended to do away with the animal but all he had was a knife and he had developed a strange attachment to Wolf and really did not know if he could put him down. Carr offered to do it for him and Morgan said to give him a few days and he would be back and let him take care of it.

CHAPTER 4

A Mere Soldier

Rueben Persinger lived up the mountain holler about three miles above the Eggleston place with his wife Della and two black and tan hounds named Pete and Repete. His cabin was built into the side of a cliff with a back door that opened in to a cave. The one room cabin had a kitchen with a slab table and the other end was a sitting area with two chairs and a settee made from wild cherry limbs. These were twisted green in the shape needed for the bench, back and legs. When they dried out they were as tough as if he had used iron. The three bedrooms were back in the cave. The first room was larger that the whole front of the house with two more rooms down the nature made hall. Della had furnished each room with a home made bed and twisted wood bureau made by Rueben. They only used the front bedroom now that their children were gone. Delta married off and Donald off to the big war. In the dead of winter she had taken to letting the hounds sleep in the corridor that connected the three bedrooms. The temperature in the cave was a constant sixty two degrees year round. They never needed heat, just two quilts on the bed and they slept that way all year, winter and summer.

Rueben was seventy one years old and Della was sixty one, they had lived in the cave house for 43 years and raised their children there. Delta lived with her husband and three children about three miles away as the crow flies in the Vier's Settlement. They visited regularly and maintained a close relationship. Donald had been drafted into the army in the summer of 1863, he was only eighteen years old when he left. He had been captured at the battle of Kernstown and had been in a Yankee prison in Elmira, New York since the previous September. Delta prayed for him every day and could not understand, if he was alright why he had not made it home, since the war had been over for two months now. She looked for him every day to come walking up the rocky road to the cliff side home. So far, she had not heard hide nor hair from him and it was grating on her nerves more every day. She found herself being short with Rueben and the hounds.

He told her one morning he was going to go down to the Eggleston place and see if he had made it home from the war. Perhaps Morgan would have some information about Donald if he had. He had caught a nice mess of trout the day before at the Blue Hole and still had several left over from the previous night's supper. He sometimes kept them in a trap he had made that let fresh water in on them and kept them alive as they were placed at the edge of the creek. That way he did not have to eat them all at once just because he had made a good catch. He decided he would take four of them on a wooden stringer cut from a branch down to the Eggleston's. If Morgan was not there then his wife could eat them.

Persinger was whistling as he turned up the lane to Morgan and Maggie Eggleston's place. The whistle turned in to a gasp as he neared the porch of the little shack. Someone, he guessed Morgan, in a gray Confederate uniform was on his back flat on the ground with a huge grey wolf looking animal on top of him. The handle of a knife protruded from the chest of the animal. What had been a face on the poor man was a mass of torn flesh with black flies swarming around and in it. The body appeared swollen and decay had obviously started with the accompanying smell. Poor Rueben was shocked beyond belief at the carnage before him. He stumbled against the steps risers and looked up at the open front door. Inside the living room he could see a woman's legs protruding under a kitchen chair. With a cry of surprise and anguish he looked in enough to recognize the swollen face and green eyes, now turning black, of Maggie Eggleston. Where her lovely slender neck had been was now a few bones, tendons and leaders. A huge pool of blood surrounded her bright red hair. A swarm of black flies buzzed around her head also. With a gag and retching sound Persinger stumbled to the porch and threw up over the railing. When his stomach stopped heaving he clomped down the steps and around the body of Morgan and the wolf and ran screaming down the lane as fast as his arthritic legs could carry him.

He ran all the way to the village, shrieking and babbling to himself like a madman. He ran right past four houses and didn't even think of stopping. He needed to get to the hotel and store and mill, where they might be enough people to hear this awful news. He wished he lived in a big city where it would be possible to assemble enough ears to hear what he had to tell them. The horror he had witnessed was too great for so small a number of people as he would find in the village. He must find someone important enough to share this news with. He ran right past a Rebel soldier trudging north just above the hotel. He never even glanced at the dirty gray clad figure. A mere soldier, he could not waste this news on a mere soldier.

"Dad, Dad what's wrong? Dad, Dad stop where are you going? Stop, stop, Dad."

He turned and saw Donald standing there with concern etched in his tired bearded face.

"Dad what's happened? Is it Mom?"

"No son, it's not your Mom. It's the Eggleston's. They are both dead, a wolf killed them both. Oh, it's awful. Come on." He hurried on down the road past the hotel screaming.

Two men came from the hotel and three from the store, one of them Carr, to see what had happened to Mr. Persinger. He babbled out the news of finding the two bodies as well as the dead wolf at the Eggleston place. He told of the condition of their throat and faces and how the wolf had obviously killed them. People began coming from all over the village and by the time he finished he had a small crowd. They began saddling their horses and hitching their wagons. Some one said to be sure and get guns as they may be more wolves in the area. Carr started to say there was only wolf around but he thought better of it and kept silent. He sent somebody to Williamsburg for the constable and they all started up the road to the Eggleston place. They also sent for Alonzo Wilson to bring two wooden coffins from his shop. When they reached what someone called the slaughterhouse they all stood transfixed at the scene. It was obvious to all that the Wolf had gotten loose some how and attacked Maggie in the kitchen and then attacked Morgan when he came to the front porch. Morgan had been able to stab the wolf through the heart before he died. Carr told of the encounter he had with Wolf six days before when Morgan had stopped at the mill on arriving back home. He said that the wolf was dangerous then and should have been put down immediately. No one could have for seen the tragedy that resulted from Morgan's hesitancy at eliminating the vicious animal. I should have shot that killer on the spot that day he lamented. No one in the crowd could blame him for not killing another man's animal even if he was vicious. That was something the wolf's owner should have handled. It was just a tragic, tragic, affair all around, everyone agreed as they milled around the yard and kitchen of the little shack.

No one knew the Eggleston's well they had not lived there for long before he left for the Confederate army. His wife stayed behind but very few people actually even knew her. The constable arrived at 2;30 that afternoon and surveyed the scene, shaking his head and muttering over and over. "What a shame, what a shame." He came to the same conclusion every one else had, that the wolf had attacked and killed them both. No one knew if the couple had any living family or not, so the constable released the bodies for burial. The stench was overpowering and there was no doubt that laying out the corpses for viewing was out of the question. He and everyone agreed that the interment should happen right away. The men loaded them in the coffins, while others commenced digging a grave on the upper end of the garden spot above the house. Reverend Rogers came and oversaw the squaring of the graves once they were opened. He was known for being able to shape the insides of the graves with a flat ended shovel with the skill of a sculpturer. He always seemed to have the knack of arriving just when the heavy digging was over and they were ready for his expertise. Many of these men were ex-soldiers and had spent years digging fortifications on the battlefields. Two six foot deep holes were a minor job for them and the graves were soon ready. They also dug a smaller hole on the other side of the house for the four legged killer and soon had him covered with the rich valley dirt.

Clarke, Nancy, Melinda and Margie were among the onlookers and Clarke and Carr helped with the graves. Alonzo Wilson etched two wooden slabs, with rest in peace. One of them said,

MORGAN A. EGGLESTON	MAGGIE EGGLESTON
Kilt by wolf June 1865	His wife, kilt to

The women cleaned the kitchen while the graves were being dug. They found some lye soap and a scrub brush and bucket and went to the well for water. They scrubbed and scrubbed and got most of the blood up from the wooden floor. Most of the onlookers were now anxious to leave for home. A prayer was said and scripture was read over the graves and then everyone left for their homes. Reuben, still visually shaken walked between his son and his wife up the road by the creek to their cave house. The little house below it with the two graves and the wooden headstones sat silent as the sun set in the west and darkness soon fell. What a tragic thing to occur just when the war was over and the young couple had the chance to settle in for the rest of their lives together. No post war babies would play in the front yard and in the creek out back when no mountain rain had fallen and the stream was a placid and peaceful brook whose cool waters would refresh them on a hot summer's day. All of the future gone, because of the sudden attack of the wild animal he had rescued.

Donald Persinger was glad to be home from the war. He had spent seven months in the prison at Elmira, New York and he knew he was lucky to be alive. He had been captured under very unlucky circumstances at a Confederate victory, rout actually, at the battle of Kernstown. Even though he could see the steeples of the Winchester churches and he was that close to the larger town the battle was named for the small village. He was in Company A of the 22nd Virginia Infantry and they were pushing the Yanks back down the valley. In a dead run they chased the fleeing Union troops. Donald had always been a very fast runner and he got so far out in front of the rest of his company that he ran smack into the Yankee lines that had stopped and formed a line of battle just before the bridge crossed the Shenandoah River. He went over a rise and not twenty feet away were a hundred or more bluecoats waiting for the gray advance. He was by himself and running so hard that he passed right in to their lines before he could stop himself. He had appeared so quickly that the blue soldiers did not have time to even raise their guns to shoot him. A quick thinking corporal just stuck out his foot and Donald went flying and landed on his stomach in the wet grass. Before he could gain his feet, four Yankees had him in their clutches, one of them got him in a headlock and he soon stopped struggling. When they pulled out to cross the bridge, he was with them under guard. He stood by helplessly and watched them set the bridge afire.

A cold bitter winter faced him with little to eat and minimal shelter from the freezing temperatures that never seemed to warm above freezing. When the war was finally over the U.S. government gave them a choice, take the oath to the United States and they would receive a train ticket home or they could walk home if they could. He knew that in his weak condition he could not stand the long walk home to southern West Virginia but he stubbornly refused to take the oath. After languishing there until the first of June he finally took the oath and headed south on a loaded troop train. He came south through the Shenandoah Valley that looked like a deserted burnt out district of poverty and hunger. Barns, houses and sometime small towns were empty charred shells that Sheridan had stripped of all food and shelter. Hungry families with small children were herded out just before the torches were applied to homes that had provided shelter for generations of hard working farmers. Their only crime had been to support their local government against the invading Northern armies and now the only thing they had left was their lives.

He rode the train to Covington and started the long walk to Greenbrier. Four days later he was in Lewis Mill. Just past the store he could not believe his eyes, his father was half running and stumbling toward him. He must be so glad to see me he thought and was surprised when his father ran right past him, wild eyed toward the village. He yelled to his dad and finally got his attention, the first thing Donald thought of was something must have happened to his mother. Assured it was not his mother he followed his dad to the store and listened to his tale of horror. He spent the day at the Eggleston place, helping with the grave digging and the burial of the two poor souls.

That first night his mother was overjoyed to see her son back home and fixed him a meal of ham, mashed potatoes and a leek type of green that grew only on the north side of the mountains. They had a very pungent odor that lingered with the person who ate them for days. Mountain people swore by them as a spring tonic and every one in a household usually ended up eating them as that was the only way all family members could stand the smell. They were called ramps and were only available from early spring to June.

The events of the day were on everyone's mind and dampened the joy of Donald's home coming. Conversation was subdued because everyone's mind would drift back to the events at the little house in the dale below them and it everyone had trouble concentrating on the topic at hand. His mother was still glad to see him and so was his father, although, he still seemed to be in shock over the day's events. Donald's fatigue drove him to the little cave bedroom in the back shortly after he ate. He asked his mother to allow him to sleep as long as he could and she complied. He slept all that night and the next day, arose for a small bite to eat and slept through until the next afternoon. When he at last awoke he was famished and ate bowl after wooden bowl of the soup his mother had made that morning. He took a bath in the creek and changed from the rags he had worn since December to civilian clothes he found in the wild cherry chest in his old bedroom.

He sat on the front porch with his father and they both smoked corn cob pipes as daylight began to fade and the owls cried in the trees across the creek. He asked his father if the Cutlip family still lived in the next holler over. He really wanted to know about Cassie, the youngest daughter, but felt he should inquire about the whole family. His father answered that they were still there. He said the oldest boy James had been killed at Petersburg and Lillian the oldest girl had married and left the area. But, the two other girls and a boy were still with the parents on the little farm. Donald had been away in the war for three years and thought about Cassie Cutlip almost every night he was gone. He remembered the last time he saw her, it was the night before he left for the army. He had known her all his life but it was like he saw her for the first time that night. There had been a dance at the Watson house that night and she was there wearing a blue gingham dress. He remembered the way her blonde curls bounced up and down to the rhythm of her feet as she swirled in the light of the lanterns. He was a bit shy when it came to dancing and he was taken aback when she brushed off the other lads who were following her like a dog pack and came directly to him.

"Come on Donald, let's dance." She said as she grabbed his hand and dragged him toward the dance floor. He hopped up and down, from one foot to the other like a turkey gobbler in the spring, for a few seconds. Then he seemed to kind of get the hang of it. They whirled around and around then went through the various twists and turns in response to the figure caller's commands. He liked the feel of her arms around him and the soft warmth of her hand in his. She tilted her head up to look at him and laughed happily as they swirled to the music. Her blue eyes and full mouth had filled his thoughts many times in the last lonely years.

He was in luck, the next tune they played was a slow one and she seemed to fit perfectly in his arms. They talked and he told her he was leaving for a soldier the next morning. He told her he could not believe they had not noticed each other before that night. She gave him a deep kiss when the night was over. She told him to be careful so they could dance again when he got back. He wondered if she had thought of him the last years or did she have someone else. Had he longed for someone who had forgotten him as soon as the next dance was held? He resolved to find out the next morning. He would go up to the Cutlip place and find out for himself if she still remembered him. He would see if she was the girl of his dreams or if she just felt sorry for a poor soldier who was leaving for battle? Maybe, she kissed all the soldier's like that when they left for the army. His pride and memories would not allow him to think that, he was going to see her the next morning. He fell asleep after he had resolved to see her the next day.

Donald ate breakfast with his parents the next morning and waited until 10:00 when the sun was high in the morning sky to go for his visit to the Cutlip place. He walked out to the main road and turned up the mountain. The cabin sat off the road in a small valley that had just enough cleared land for a garden and enough pasture for the two milk cows that supplied the family with milk, cream and butter. The Cutlips were known locally for their schmeirkase, a form of cottage cheese made from slightly sour curds and added cream. They sold it to the store in the village and had for decades.

As Donald approached the gate that crossed the lane leading to the house he glanced at the brier thicket that grew around the gate post and up the side of the hill, all the way to the wood line. He could see someone wearing blue moving slightly in the berry filled brier patch.

"Hello", he called out." Hello in the berry patch."

He was answered with a lilting female voice.

"Hello, yourself. Who's that down in the road?" The voice moved closer to him as the words were spoken and he soon saw a blonde head of curls appear as she picked her way gingerly down the path toward him through the clinging briers. She had a wooden bucket filled to the top with the huge blackberries that grew in profusion in the brier thicket. She squeezed past the last prickly brier and straightened up to see who this was visiting on a warm summer morning. A smile lit up her face when she saw who the visitor was.

"Well, well, well," Cassie said slowly, " Donald's finally back from the war and in one piece too, it looks like." She looked him up and down coyly.

"Hello Cassie, you are just as pretty as I remembered you all those nights since I've been gone." He noticed she was wearing the same blue gingham dress she had worn at the dance that night three years ago. It was obvious it had been demoted to everyday wear now. She had been sneaking a bite of blackberries because she had just a faint stain still left on her mouth. The dark stain seemed to highlight the fullness of her lips. He found himself wanting to kiss those lips. They talked of his return and the terrible scene at the shack in the dale. She said she could not bring herself to go see the carnage the wolf had wrought on her neighbors. He carried her bucket of berries to the house with her. Her mother, sister and brother were there. She said her father was in the mountains on a trout fishing trip with her uncles and would be back in two days.

He ate dinner with the family and Cassie's mother made a black berry cobbler she served with thick whipped cream that Cassie's sister Opel had made. While waiting for the food to be prepared he and Cassie sat on the front porch in side by side rocking chairs. He steered the conversation to the last night he had seen her and told her how he had cherished that night's memory. Unable to wait any longer he asked her if she was seeing any one else. She answered that she was not now seeing anyone. Reluctantly, she informed him that she had been seeing Nathan Barksdale from Spring Creek but that he had been killed in the battle of New Market over a year ago. She said the two of them should take it easy and enjoy each others company and see what happened.

He spent the whole day at Cassie's house and started home just before dark with a promise he could return the next day. His father and mother were on the porch of the cave house when he returned. "You must have found a warm seat at the Cutlips." His father drawled as he greeted them. Donald told them he had been thinking of Cassie the entire time he was in the war and he intended to marry her as soon as he could get her to say yes. His mother said she was a fine girl and would make him a good wife if he was lucky enough to get a yes when he asked the question. He would spend so much time with her that she might even ask him, he said with a laugh. He did spend time with her, nearly every day for forty seven days and she gave him the yes answer he was looking for on the third time he asked. They planned their wedding for mid-July and both anxiously awaited the date.

CHAPTER 5

Where's Bill? Don't You Lie.

Basil Winslow was worried about his brother Bill. He had not been seen for more than 3 weeks and his absence was strange considering their business in real estate was keeping all the brothers busy. He felt like Bill who was more aggressive than the other brothers, except Basil, would not miss the chance to make the profits that were making them all rich. Basil and his four brothers were from the slums of Wheeling and each had spent some time in the Union army. They had a difficult time with authority though and every one of the Winslow brothers had been cashiered out of the army for some reason or another. Their reasons differed as much as their personalities, Bill, stole a Colonel's horse and Basil for leaving his unit to play poker. The youngest one Ross had killed a fellow private over a piece of hardtack. Samuel and Lawrence had deserted in the face of the enemy at the battle of Monocacy and walked home to Wheeling. When the army sent a sergeant looking for them they simply cut his throat in the alley and stripped his uniform from him and later burned it. They threw his naked unidentifiable body in the Ohio River and chortling, slapped each other on the back as the swift current sent his body south.

They had moved south to Greenbrier the previous November and now made their residence in the back of a tavern at Frankford known as the Double Cross. They had stopped there one day and Lawrence said he liked the place. They persuaded the proprietor an elderly lady named Audrey that she should sell out to them. The transaction was surprisingly easy, Bill slapped her twice and Basil once and she took the hundred dollars they gave her and signed the bill of sale. They practically threw her out and tore the AUDREY"S sign off the building, turned it around and wrote DOUBLE CROSS on the back and nailed it back up. The place had room in the back to sleep, eat and play poker and they soon settled in to their new home. Lawrence ran the tavern in the front and the other four ran their strong arm real estate business out of the back.

The Winslow's were backed by three of Wheelings leading citizens and politicians. The brother's business practices were really quite simple they forced the desolated Confederates by force and coercion to sell them their farms and land. Of course, the price was always at a bargain level and the brothers would net thirty percent of the selling price. They would get fifteen percent from the sellers and fifteen from the buyers. The backers were happy because they were getting land at unbelievable prices and there was nothing the sellers could do about their plight. Take what the Winslow's offered or be killed, was the only two choices they had. They always took the offer after some persuasion. The brothers soon had more money than they ever knew existed. They frequented the shops in Lewisburg and dressed in the very finest clothing and rode the best horses. Nothing seemed to be too expensive for them and if they could not find what they wanted in the shops in town they would have them order it.

When Bill had been gone nearly a month, Basil called the brothers together and told them it was time to find Bill. They knew he had found a woman to spend time with whose husband was away in the Confederate army. He had divulged little to them about her. He would be away sometimes for two or three days but never longer than that. Basil had thought when he did not come back this time that he had just settled in with her for awhile. One thing he knew, Bill had always been able to take care of himself, but he had been gone to long this time. The four mounted up and rode out the Williamsburg road toward the village of Lewis Mill near the foot of Cold Knob Mountain. They pooled their tiny bit of information that Bill had told each one over the last six months. It seemed the only thing they knew was the girl's place was on a creek above Lewis Mill, somewhere off the road to Richwood. They did not know if it was to the left or right of the road, only that it was a cabin or shack on a creek.

They rode up the valley to the little settlement, past the church and blacksmith shop. Then they rounded the turn to the store and mill, three loafers were sunning them selves on the wooden benches. They looked at the four riders with apprehension, as the Winslow's seemed, despite their impeccable dress and fine saddles and mounts to exude evil. Heavily armed, they seemed out of place for this small town, even though a number of well dressed business men traveled the road and stayed at the hotel just above the copse of oak trees beside the store. These travelers looked as if their tailored clothes did not fit them. The expensive clothing fit their trim bodies perfectly in a physical way but some how made one think of how a bum would look in a tailored suit, kind of out of place. Even these backwoods loafers could tell that the brothers were not in any way, gentlemen. The Winslow's didn't dismount but on their horses they were eye level with the bench sitters.

Basil did not waste time with pleasant greetings, he started right in with:

"We are looking for our brother he has been in these hills for nearly a month. He's about five foot ten, medium build, sandy colored hair and rides a black gelding. Have you seen him, and don't you lie?" his eyes narrowed.

The three locals looked at each other nervously and answered quickly that they had not seen anyone matching that description. Each one was treated to the hard stares of the brothers and again repeated that they knew no one like that.

"He would have been visiting a young lady who lives up this road somewhere. Her husband was off in the secesh army and could have been killed, we hope so anyway. We want directions to any wench that lives on a creek and had a man off in the Reb army committing treason. Speak up and don't stutter," barked Basil.

"Mister, everyone who lives up this road, almost all fought for the South. This road goes all the way to Nicholas County and we don't know all of the people," one of the men stammered.

"Yea," another one chimed in, "Every one of the hollers has some kind of a creek up it and nearly every one has a shack on it, most a lot more than one. Honest we don't know which one it could be."

Melinda heard the menacing tone of Basil's voice and the concern and rising fear in the voice's of the three locals and started toward the front porch to see what was happening. Carr and Clarke had left early that morning for Covington to return two mules Clarke had borrowed from someone when the war ended. They planned to make the trip on returning, down the river to Alderson to a wholesale house for store supplies. They would not be back for three days. She was accustomed to operating a business by her self though and hurriedly opened the door and stepped out to the porch.

She was taken aback to see the four riders mounted just at the edge of the stores porch. She felt a chill down her back as she looked in to the eyes of the four horsemen. They had such a coldness to them and they looked her up and down in a way that made her feel like she was standing naked before them.

"What is it you men were looking for," she asked in an even voice that surprised her, as her insides were quaking.

Basil curtly repeated what he had said to the others, but added he thought they were lying to him. She assured him that they were not lying and she did not know anyone in the mountains as she was new to the area. She stared at him coldly and said if that was all they needed they could ride on. They treated themselves to another long look at her perceived nakedness and abruptly turned their horses in to the road and kicked them in to a trot. They went up the mountain road past the hotel and were soon out of sight.

"That's a rough bunch if there ever was one," said one of the locals.

They talked about where the missing brother could have been hanging out and they came up with four different women up that road who had spent the war years without their husbands. They all agreed that was just the ones they knew of and they were sure that there were others.

The four riders continued up the Cold Knob road past several houses. As they rode they talked about the woman at the store and how she had stared them down. One of them made the comment that they were all thinking, what a sight she was when she came out of the store to face them down. Lawrence said that he knew she had not seen Bill or their brother would have owned a store by now. No way would he pass her up for a cabin up a creek. They took the first road on the left and turned down the narrow lane to a little shack that had a deserted look. Basil yelled out and when no one appeared they dismounted and looked around. The house was empty and looked like no one had been there for a while. Ross went to the well for water and stubbed his boot toe on something that was heavy and didn't move much. He reached down and picked up a household iron. It looked clean and free of rust like it may have been inside recently. He thought, someone gave up on the wrinkles and this homestead. He laid the iron on the wooden ledge that surrounded the well opening and lowered the bucket. They watered themselves and took the horses to the stream that was not real close to the house. Lawrence said he wondered why they had dug the well with the stream available and surmised that the creek had probably gone dry sometime in the past. Sam said he did not know and did not care one way or the other. He had no patience for reasoning and wondering why things were, he just took things as they came. He left deep thinking to others and spied some apples hanging on a tree at the end of the garden spot. He was enjoying one when he found the new graves and hollered for the others. They read the headstones with the Killed by a Wolf engraving on them and said they did not even think there were wolves still around these parts. Basil said it was time for them to move, they would find a house nearby and ask questions there. They still needed to find Bill.

The smoke from the cave house fireplace was rising as they rode in to the small cleared yard. Reuben and Donald came out of the house in response to Basil's yell. Ignoring the Winslow's menacing attitudes they answered truthfully that they knew nothing of the brother they were looking for. Their open candor must have satisfied Basil that they were being truthful. He wanted to know who lived up the road. They told him of the Cutlip homestead and that the only other home up the road belonged to Mr. Miller, an elderly man who recently lost his wife and lived alone. Basil wanted to know if Miller's wife had been killed by wolves. He was told she died of quinsy. Donald then told about the Eggleston's and how they had been killed by a vicious attack animal, half dog-half wolf that he brought back from the army with him. This animal had been used for chasing deserters and run away slaves and that it was trained to kill. He guessed it went wild on them. Morgan had managed to kill the dog with his knife as it attacked him. They abruptly turned their horses before he finished talking and rode out without a goodbye or other word to them. Donald told his father the brothers were cold blooded killers and assholes and he hoped they never saw them again.

CHAPTER 6

Out of Control

As the searchers rounded a bend in the main road they met a man on foot walking south. His name was Carl Blake and he was an accommodating fellow who was always willing to help anyone any time. He was surprised by the attitude of the Winslow brothers. Basil was in a ill mood and demanded to know who he was and where he was going. When Carl told him his name and that he was going to the village, Basil asked if he knew Bill Winslow and proceeded to curse and abuse him when he answered negatively. He took a rope that he had on his saddle and began suddenly beating Carl with it. The viciousness of the attack from the stranger on the horse above him soon bloodied Carl and caused him to roll in to the ditch in a ball with his arms around his head to protect his face. The blows eventually subsided and panting from his efforts Basil and the brothers left the poor beaten fellow and proceeded on up the dusty road. Carl stumbled from the ditch after a while and made his way to the creek by the road and washed the blood from his face and head. He could not for the life of him figure what he had done to set the lunatic on the horse in to such a rage to beat him so. He lay on the cool grass by the creek and soon dropped of to sleep.

The next feeder road the riders came to went off to the right and crossed the creek. Heavy laurel thickets in full bloom covered the right of the road and limestone cliffs rose steeply on the left. The pink rhododendron blossoms were everywhere in the thickets and gave off a fresh flowery scent that was lost on the four rough necks who were now on a mission to find their brother and partner in crime. They rounded a bend and came on a cabin on the right of the road with a stream flowing in front of it. They dismounted and let the horses drink from the stream. This had to be the place they agreed, stream, cabin and now lets find the woman. Basil went in to the yard and yelled toward the house. After a moment the door was opened by a slim auburn haired young woman who greeted them with an open expression, not especially friendly but not unfriendly either and asked if she could help them in some way.

"Yeah, you can. Where's Bill?" Basil growled.

"There ain't no Bill around here," the young woman answered.

"What's your name lady," he again barked in her direction. She said that her name was Nancy Lewis and repeated that no one named Bill was around. He told her that their brother had been spending some time with a lady at a place that he described that matched this one to a t. He said they were going to look around and demanded to know where her man was. She said he would be back shortly and that she did not like the men's attitude toward her and her husband would not like it either when he returned. She kept to her self that her husband was gone for three days.

Sam, Ross and Lawrence began looking in the out buildings while Basil bounded up the steps, brushed Nancy aside and entered the cabin. He walked around looking at every thing and asked Nancy if her husband had been in the Confederate army. She said yes he had. Then he demanded to know when he came home from the war and Lawrence burst in the door before she could answer. He informed Basil that there was a fresh grave on the knoll above the house. He wanted to know who was in the grave and Nancy stammered as she tried to remember who was buried there. After a pause, she told him that she and her husband had just married and neither knew who was buried in that grave on the knoll. The man named Basil became more and more agitated, he paced the floor and ran his hands through his hair and looked at her wild-eyed. He began talking, half to himself and half to his brothers. The more he talked the more convinced he was that his brother Bill was buried in the grave on the hill. He said that he could see it all now , she and Bill had been carrying on and her husband had come home from the war and either her husband had killed Bill or they had done it together. He had the others begin to look all through the house for something that was Bill's. They ransacked every drawer or corner and were convinced they would find something that would solve the mystery of Bill's disappearance. Basil again asked where her husband was. Nancy was afraid if she told him he was gone for three days they would never leave so she stuck to her story that he was close by and would be here any time.

She tried to convince the madmen that she had married her husband after the war was over and that she had just moved there from Monroe County. There was no reasoning with this bunch of marauders however, for Basil suddenly slapped her across the cheek and forced her outside. He said that he would bring her husband home and told the others to burn the house. Oil lamps were thrown against the walls and flaring matches soon had the house blazing. While Nancy sobbed and cursed the Winslow's, Basil just laughed like a lunatic and stared at the flames as they roared all through the house and the black smoke rolled skyward. He screamed over the roar of the fire, "This will bring your husband and when he comes I will kill him."

Custus McClung was on his veranda at Twin Sugar when he saw the black smoke boiling up from the holler down at the foot of the mountain. He had lived there for sixty nine years and could easily see that the smoke was coming from

Clarke's place. The heavy smoke in such a concentrated area had to be the house burning and he knew that Clarke was away for a few days. His high wheeled carriage stood with his two horses hitched just off the veranda as he was just about to leave for a trip down the mountain to Williamsburg. He yelled at Luther and several other workers who were down at the barn to bring all the buckets they could find, that Clarke's house was burning. He started down the mountain in a run with the carriage bumping wildly on some of the larger ruts. He had put off some badly needed work on the mountain shale road. He passed Carr's house on the right of the road in a sharp turn and hurried on down to the burning cabin. As he got closer he could smell the burning chestnut and cedar logs in the seasoned highly flammable wooden structure. When he passed the small barn he could see all the way down to the house. Four men were dismounted in the yard and one was holding a struggling Nancy by her waist. She was screaming and trying her best to break away from a wild looking man who had his head tilted back and was laughing insanely in a high pitched tone that could be heard even at that distance above the roar of the flames.

Just as he had done all his life Custus held no thoughts for his own safety and never reined up his horses at all until he reached the front yard of the burning house.

"What is going on here?" he asked as his high wheeled buggy came to a sliding halt.

He was pulling out the double barrel shot gun he kept behind the seat for emergencies with his right hand and holding the reins in his left. Basil shot first, followed closely by Sammie and Lawrence, all three missed with their first pistol shot and Custus turned the shot gun toward them. Sam was caught with the first barrel of the shot gun, through the throat and upper chest. He went backward with both feet in the air in front of him, his arms flew up and out as if he was doing toe touches. Custus's second shot was low and caught Ross in the lower leg below the knee. The deep brown of his thigh high leather boots were instantly speckled with red holes from the knee to the instep and pieces of the fine leather were splayed across the cabin's yard behind him.

Ross was able to get a shot off with his pistol just as the shotgun's blast hit him. His, Lawrence's and Basil's pistol shots all three hit Custus in the chest. His silk vest caught the bullets and pushed him back in to the soft leather of his carriage. He was killed instantly and his head rocked left to right as his nervous horses danced in their traces. He had tried to help his neighbor just as he always had and this time his generosity had cost him his life. Ross split the air with his screams of pain and anguish. The gunfire had quieted Basil's laughter and he ordered Lawrence to help get Ross on his horse. He could see two wagons coming down from the mountain, loaded with men to fight the fire. He gave Nancy a shove to the ground and mounted up. They quickly rode down the road and out of sight around the turn. Nancy sobbed as the wagons pulled in to the yard and everyone stood and gaped at the two dead men, a crying woman and a house fire that was too far gone to extinguish.

Carl Blake lay on the grass by the creek and heard riders coming fast down the road. His head had stopped paining him although his face still smarted from the blows from the folded rope. The cold water from the creek had seemed to ease it a bit. Three riders came thundering by him as he hugged the bank to keep from being seen. It was the man who had beat him and two of the others who had been with him. They're missing one, he thought. The one who was behind and seemed to be the youngest was crying out in pain, as he bounced along in the saddle. His boot from the knee down seemed awash with fresh blood that had coated his horses belly a bright red. They had been in a fight somewhere obviously and one had been wounded pretty badly and the other one might be dead.

He crawled up the bank, over the ditch and stood up in the road. As he did he could see smoke rising from up the mountain to the right and knew something substantial, barn or house was obviously on fire. He hurried up the road and crossed the creek up the holler road that lead to Twin Sugars.

He knew the fire was well below there. It had to be at one of the Lewis brothers places. He could hear the roar of the flames before he rounded the turn.

The sight before him was something he knew he would never forget. Clarke's new wife was sitting on the bed of a wagon, shaking her head sideways over and over. Mr. McClung was sitting dead in the leather seat of his buggy. The fourth of the ruffians who had beat him was laying dead on the ground with his gun still clutched in his dead cold hands. Eight of McClung's former slaves were standing looking at the scene or pacing back and forth. They seemed to be glad to see a live white man without a gun. None of them could believe the scene they had ridden up on.

"What on earth, was this about?" Carl asked anyone who would answer. Nancy tried to explain what had transpired. She told of the four men who had ransacked their house and that they were convinced the grave on the knoll was their missing brother's grave. She said they thought she had been having an affair with their brother and that Clarke had come back from the war and killed him. They had burned the house so Clarke would see it and rush home. She had lied to them that he was close by. Instead poor Mr. McClung had seen the smoke and came rushing down to help. Before they could kill him he killed that brother there and wounded another one. The bad men had shot first and he only returned their fire with the shotgun. The telling of the events seemed to wear Nancy out and she began sobbing again. Carl told of the encounter he had with the Winslow' and the beating he had taken from the leader who seemed to be a wild man.

"What can we do to help?" asked Mason, who had been Mr. McCLung's favorite slave and since the war's end stayed on with him to work the plantation as a free hired hand.

"We will try to keep the fire offen the out buildings. After that I don't know what we should do next," he stated in an earnest tone.

Carl scratched his head and asked, "do you have an icehouse on the plantation"? Mason answered, yes they did.

They decided to load McClung's body on one of the wagons and take it to the icehouse on the mountain. They did not want the killer's body placed in the same place as Custus's. So they moved it to the small icehouse Clarke had build in the hill side behind the burning cabin. They knew they should not bury it before the sheriff came to investigate the shootings.

The cabin blaze began to sub side, the roof and walls had fallen inward, only the chimney made from the Roaring Creek rocks was still standing. It would stand as a lone sentinel over the ashes for years to come, like a guard on his post through wind, rain and snow. Nancy had never met Custus's daughter or son-in-law. Clarke had told her they lived in Covington and he was a lawyer. She asked if any of the men knew where the house was in Covington and Mason stated that he had been there and could find the place. It was decided that Carl would take Nancy to the village to stay with Margie. She would stay there until Clarke came back. Mason would take the high wheeled buggy and go to Covington to tell his daughter of the tragedy. Another of the former slaves, Albert, would take one of the wagons and go to Williamsburg to alert the constable. He was asked to tell the constable that one of the attackers had been wounded badly in the lower leg and see if he had sought medical attention at either of the two doctors in that town.

Mason objected to taking the high wheeled buggy with the blood and three bullet holes in it that far from home. A Negro in a fancy rig like that with bullet holes could get him hung. He said he would rather take Mr. McClung's larger carriage that could carry six people and said he would like Carl to accompany him in even that. Carl and Nancy agreed that made sense and would be better for all concerned. She cautioned them to be on the lookout for Carr and Clarke as they had left before daylight that morning for Covington and perhaps they would see them somewhere on the road coming back to Greenbrier. Mason left with the small buggy to Twin Sugar's to get the much larger four horse carriage, he planned to pick up Carl at Margie's in the village. They rode with Albert in the wagon to Margie's place in the village while the other men stayed to watch the dying fire. Nancy took a last look at the pile of timbers and embers that just a short time ago had been their happy home in the holler. She could not stifle the bitter tears that rose in her eyes as she thought of what poor Clarke's reaction to this awful news would be.

Melinda saw the wagon with Nancy, a Negro and Carl Blake as it passed the store. She ran to the porch and saw it stop at her Aunt Margie's house down the road. She watched as Margie ran and embraced her and helped her down from the wagon seat and across the yard. Melinda quickly ran inside, grabbed her keys and locked the store. She reached Margie's house quickly and listened to Nancy and Carl's story. Shocked at the news, she hugged and rocked Nancy back and forth as she listened to the details of the animal's fury and violence perpetrated on a poor girl alone at her home. She knew it had been the four horsemen that she had stared down at the store that morning. Carl confirmed it with his tale of being beaten by the rope of the leader. Mason soon arrived with the four horse carriage and Carl left with him. The women implored them to please look out for Clarke and Carr on their journey as he crossed the yard to the carriage.

Carr and Clarke Lewis had left before daylight that morning in a wagon pulled by two mules, with two more tied behind it. These two were to be returned to Ellsworth Collins, a friend from the 22nd Va. Infantry who had loaned them to him back in March when they had passed through Covington on the way to Lewis Mill. He had been in Point Lookout Prison with Clarke. The brothers talked of many things on the road that trip. Carr told Clarke that he planned to ask Melinda to marry him. They stopped in Lewisburg and he purchased a wedding band for the two of them. He had to guess at Melinda's ring size, he was able to try his until he found one that fit. They spent two hours in town and then headed over the James River and Kanawha Turnpike toward Covington. They reached that place at 9:30 that night and Clarke was disappointed to hear that Ellsworth was away on a horse buying trip to Indiana. This information was given to them by his barn manager there in

Covington. They being rather tired were happy to sleep in the barn after a dinner of dried beef and crackers they had packed with them. The next morning found them at a small café in the downtown area eating ham and eggs. Clarke had left a note for Ellsworth expressing his thanks for the loan of the mules and the hospitality of the barn. Carr being the new business man that he had become insisted the barn manager sign that he had received the two mules in good condition. While eating breakfast, the subject of Custus McClung's daughter, Mabel Morgan, living there came up and they decided to go by and visit with her while they were there.

The café owner knew the Morgan's and directed them to their house. They were clopping along down the street they lived on when a four horse carriage over took them at a high rate of speed. Some one yelled out Clarke's name and he was surprised to see Carl Blake from Lewis Mill leaning down to wave him over. Carl hopped down from the roadster's seat as soon as Mason could stop the horses. He looked very tired but excited also, a combination of expressions that alerted Clarke more than his just being there that something was very wrong.

"I have some bad news for you," he blurted out without hesitating. "Some crazy Yankee rough necks came to the village looking for a brother that they said was missing. They roughed me up with a rope and then went to your house. They thought that fresh grave on the knoll by your baby's was their brother's. Nancy ain't really hurt, but they slapped her a little. Then they burned your house down, right to the ground. Mr. McClung saw the smoke and come runnin' They shot at him and missed and he killed one and wounded another one. They shot him three times in the chest, killed him dead. We are on our way to tell Mabel about her daddy. I took Nancy to Margie's and she and Melinda are taking care of her. She ain't hurt just upset over all this," he suddenly seemed to run out of steam and bent over gasping for breath like a winded horse.

"Oh, my, my, " said Clarke. " And all this happened yesterday?"

"Yes, sir" panted Carl. "About 11:00 yesterday, We left for here about three o'clock and we stopped about four hours last night to rest these horses."

"What kind of trash are these people? You say they beat you too."

"With a rope they did, like a dog, and for no reason, they're just mean as all get out. I'll tell you, just plain mean. They should be hung for what they did to Mr. McClung, he was the nicest man in the county. "said Carl.

They went on up the hill to the residence of Mabel and John Morgan, all regretting what they would have to tell her. The house was large and well kept with white painted brick and red shutters. The wagon and the carriage carrying the four men must have been heard from inside because the front door opened and there stood Mabel looking at them in surprise. She seemed glad to see them all and they realized that something had to be wrong for them to be there with her father's large carriage with out him. They all seemed to try to clear their throats and looked down at their feet and avoided her eyes. Then Carr stepped forward and told Mabel that there had been a shooting and some bad men had shot her father and that he had died the day before. She stammered something about this must all be a mistake and fainted dead away. Carr was close enough to grab her and steer her to a bench beside the doorway before she fell to the bricks on the portico. A colored lady came to the door immediately and tried to revive her from her faint. A girl of about ten appeared, then ran in to the house and returned with a glass of water. She sprinkled some on Mabel's face and she soon came around. She sent for John at his office and Carl and Mason went to the kitchen for food. They had not eaten since the morning before and had no desire for food after the days happening until they had awoke in the early morning hours.

John Morgan sent one of the servants to exchange the four tired horses for fresh ones. The family packed for the trip to the mountains and soon realized they would need to take a second carriage to carry the luggage and all of the passengers.

It was decided that Carr and Clarke would start back right away in the wagon pulled by the mules. The Morgan's with their three children and all the luggage would come in the two carriages, one driven by Mason, the other by Carl Blake. Those two could get some sleep and they could all start at first light the next morning.

When the Winslow's rode back down the valley they were anxious to get Ross to a doctor. He cried out in pain and the blood continued to flow down his stirrup to his horse's belly. Lawrence called to Basil that they had to get him off the horse or he would bleed to death. Just as he had stated this they came up on an elderly man in a buggy who was barely moving down the dusty road. Basil came up beside him and ordered him to stop the buggy and to step down on the road. Ross was placed in the buggy and Lawrence took the reins out of the protesting man's hands.

"Where's the nearest doctor?" demanded Basil.

"At Williamsburg, two doors down from the livery stable" said the old man haltingly.

"Get out of the way," Lawrence ordered as he slapped the horse's rear and the buggy jolted forward. Basil grabbed the reins of the two saddled mounts and kicked out at the man standing in the road. His boot just missed the cheek of the newly made pedestrian and knocked his hat into the ditch. The man was soon left behind as the brother's mad dash to medical help renewed. They wheeled in to the front yard of the large white house with the doctor's sign in front. Basil hammered on the door with his fist and Lawrence helped Ross who hopped on one leg to the porch of the residence. The door was opened by a man in a white shirt with black vest who answered affirmatively to Basil's barked question of was he a doctor. The doctor elevated the lower part of Ross's leg and cut the pants leg and removed the boot of the moaning patient. It took him nearly an hour to pick the buckshot out of the numerous wounds. Ross was given laudanum for the pain. He was bandaged and ordered to stay off the leg for a week or so and keep it elevated. To the doctor's questions they turned a deaf ear as if they were not aware he was speaking to them. Basil threw him five dollars and they were soon on their way back to Frankford and their back room barroom home.

Ross drank a pint of Old Crow bourbon and soon passed out in a painless stupor. Lawrence and Basil took the buggy and horse three miles north, unhitched the horse and rolled the buggy over the steep side of the hill down to Spring Creek below. They slapped the horse on his ass and watched him run north up the pike. Murder meant nothing to them but damned if they would be hung for a horse thief.

Chapter 7
The Investigation

Carr and Clarke pushed the mules on the ride back, but still had to stop twice for two hours each to rest them. Some time late in the morning they passed right by the Double Cross tavern and turned out the Williamsburg road. They reached the house at the mill at 3:00 am and decided not to wake Nancy and the other two females. They slept for three hours and were on Margie's porch at first light.

Nancy was overjoyed to see Clarke when she was roused from sleep by their knocking at the door. Margie had given her something to relax her and she slept soundly that night. She apologized to Clarke several times before he was able to convince her that what happened at the cabin had not been her fault. She repeated the whole incident and they all were reduced to tears as she recounted the shooting of poor Custus. She told of the true bravery he had displayed as he rode right up on the four armed thugs, trying to help her. Carr was convinced they had been the same bunch he had encountered at the spring below Frankford the day he had gone to Lewisburg to see the lawyer about the transfer of the store. That day there had been five riders and it would make sense they were looking for the fifth one.

He decided right then to offer his house and farm to them. He had considered it before, now it seemed to be a necessity. They were in agreement with his plan but only until they could get the cabin in the holler rebuilt. The chance to farm the larger acreage would be much more profitable than the limited holler land could offer. They stated their desire for children and Carr grinned to himself. He knew that he could convince them to stay on permanently when their family began growing. They were grateful for the offer, it eased their minds some but they still were trying to deal with the loss of all personal items. They would be truly starting over after less than a month together.

Now that he knew his wife would be all right the anger began to set in on Clarke like a storm cloud. He could not believe that he had left his home for one day and this had happened. His life long home had been burned to the ground, his friend and neighbor killed, his wife slapped around and treated shabbily. It was too much for a man to take. He went outside and talked with Carr about going after the fellows who had done this. Carr told him they had too much to take care of with the arrangements for Custus to be attended too and keeping Nancy calm. Blake had stopped and told the sheriff of the shootings and he would be there that day. His advice was to wait and after the funeral they would go together to settle the score with the carpetbaggers.

The sheriff, constable and three deputies came up the road to Lewis Mill about eleven thirty that morning. Carr saw them approaching and flagged them down. He told them the victim was his sister in law and was inside the white house. The sheriff and constable went inside the house to interview Nancy. Carr and Clarke sat in on the discussion. She explained in a no nonsense way what had happened in the holler the day before. Clarke was proud of the way she answered their questions in frank terms, with out tears and with an absence of excess emotions. After hearing the details the sheriff asked if she could accompany them to the burned out remains of the house. They rode in a wagon behind the horsemen, to the holler. The remains of Sammie Winslow were still in the icehouse and Nancy again explained what had taken place, placing each individual where they were when Custus rode up. They looked at the body and then went to Twin Sugars to examine the remains of Custus. Nancy, Clarke and Carr stayed below at the embers of the house site while the law viewed the remains. They also looked at the buggy with the three bullet holes and examined the shot gun Custus had used on the two bad men.

Carr recognized Sammie as one of the men he had seen at the spring that day. Carl Blake had said the mean man who had beaten him had been looking for Bill Winslow. The sheriff, on returning from the plantation house, said this case looked like murder to him if Sammie Winslow had indeed fired first as Nancy insisted that he had. Arson and assault charges would also be pressed when these men were captured. Carr told him of meeting the men at the spring, what Blake had said, and Melinda identified Sammie as one of the men who had been at the store demanding information so forcibly the day before. Sheriff Knight wrote all their statements in a leather notebook he carried and assured them he would bring the perpetrators in and justice would be done. A search of the dead man turned up information identifying him as Sammie Winslow and they found an envelope addressed to him at The Double Cross Tavern at Frankford, W.V. dated just a few days before. It was from a custom saddle shop in Charleston telling him his new saddle had been sent by mule freight that day. The lawman knew where that tavern was as they had passed it just that morning. One of them had commented on the strangeness of the sign with it's almost double meaning. Two crosses had been carved in to the sign side by side. They seemed to represent one thing and the words seemed to mean some thing else, like deceit or trickery. Odd, they all had agreed. After seeing the ashes and bodies they had created they understood the sign a bit better.

Clarke stated that he would like something done with the body in his icehouse. That man had killed his good friend and neighbor and he was not looking forward to providing him with a place to spend eternity. Not above the ground in the coolness of the icehouse or below it in the dark rich dirt of the holler. He had spent his entire life here and did not want the reposing of some one who had helped abuse his wife and burn his house down mar his feelings for the place. The lawmen strapped the body across the saddle of Winslow's horse and they left for Lewisburg, They planned to get warrants for the three Winslow's as soon as they could get them signed by the judge at the courthouse. The sheriff and his deputies rode out of the holler just as the neighbors began coming from all over the surrounding hills to see for them selves if the rumors were true about the shootout at the Lewis cabin site.

Clarke, Nancy, Carr and Melinda went to Carr's house on the seventy acres above the holler. This was the first time Nancy and Melinda had seen the place. Clarke was anxious to see how Nancy would take to the house with the extra room and newness that had been missing in the cabin below. She had seemed so happy in the little cabin and now must acclimate herself to her new home. They spent about an hour there walking from room to room. After a while, Nancy seemed to be taking mental ownership of the inside of the home. She made comments about where the furniture should be moved to suit her better than its present placement. The davenport should be placed nearer the fireplace and the bed in the larger bedroom would look better here than where it presently was. The men smiled at each other when she couldn't see them and moved to the porch to allow the women the opportunity to plan changes to the interior.

The men talked about the mornings happening and agreed that the sheriff had seemed determined to bring the Winslow's to justice. Anger and determination to see Mr. McClung's murderers pay for taking his life had consumed their thoughts every since they had calmed Nancy down. If the lawmen took him in they felt sure the citizens would exact the maximum penalty for them in a jury trial. They left Carr's place after the girls finished their planning and traveled up the road to Twin Sugars. Many neighbors had gathered under the giant maple trees and were talking about the sudden happenings. The men were gathered on one end and most of the women were on the other side of the giant veranda near the separate kitchen. Some of the neighbor women were cooking and preparing food in the giant fireplace and the long wooden tables that ran down each wall of the kitchen. Aunt Rose was sitting at the head of the first table just inside the door and looked up when she saw Clarke, Carr and the two women walking across the veranda. She burst in to tears when she saw them and was obviously taking her master and friends death very, very hard. She hugged Clarke and tried to stifle her sobs long enough to be introduced to Nancy and Melinda. She kept saying she did not know what they would do with out Mr. McClung to run the plantation. They all had a good cry and everyone there that day had a heavy heart for the good man who had so brutally and abruptly been taken away from them.

The two men went to the icehouse to see Mr. McClung's cold dead body. Some one had cleaned him up and replaced his suit with the three bullet holes with one freshly pressed and cleaned. They had combed his hair and laid him in a casket made of cherry wood from the plantation. Heavy candle holders filled with large white candles were lit at each end of his coffin. They made the icehouse seem warmer than usual and gave it a softer, almost cozy feeling. The brothers gazed at the body of their good friend who had helped them in so many ways all of their lives and died still trying to help their loved one in a time of need when they themselves were not available to look out for them. They both knew they would never have a friend so dear and such a blessing again. Each vowed silently to themselves that his death would not be for nothing and his killers would know vengeance. They bid goodbye to their old friend and exited the icehouse. The Negro men who had arrived at the burning house after the murder met them when they came out. They, to a man, expressed their grief for the death of McClung and assured the brothers they would do any thing needed to help catch his killers or anything else that would help in the days to come. Clarke thanked them for coming to the aid of his wife and asked them if they had any idea who was buried in the fresh grave in the holler. They assured him that they did not know who it could be and that they had seen nothing suspicious while the brothers had been gone to the wedding or any other time.

After viewing the body the brothers and the women left the sad scene on the mountain and descended to the valley below. Darkness was beginning to fall as they reached Margie's place and she had a delicious supper of roast chicken and hot rolls from the oven waiting for them. Nancy decided to stay at Margie's for the night and Clarke went around the bend in the road with Carr to his valley home to bed down. Despite being safe at Margie's with her husband back, Nancy still thought of the events of recent days and cried herself to sleep that night. The events played over and over in her mind. She could still see the misplaced anger and hatred in Basil's face as he ordered the house to be burned. The smell of kerosene as it was splashed through out the downstairs area was not as hard as his breath had been on her cheek as he held her tightly against him and taunted that he intended to kill Clarke when he came to see what the smoke was about. She also kept thinking of the look on the face of poor Custus when the bullets had torn in to his chest. She finally fell asleep and slept fitfully as exhaustion over came her.

About noon the next day the two carriages arrived from Covington carrying the daughter of Custus with his son-in-law and grandchildren and their luggage. Carl Blake drove one carriage and Mason McClung, the former slave drove the other one. Mabel, who was quite upset at her father's death hugged Margie and was introduced to Nancy and Melinda. The funeral was tentatively set for three day's off which happened to be a Saturday. Mabel said they would bring the body to the church in the village at noon Saturday to lay in state for one hour. She had stopped in Lewisburg at the offices of the Greenbrier

Independent and given them the information for the obituary. After the service they would bury him in the family cemetery on Twin Sugars that had been the final resting place for three generations of McClungs. When the leaves were off the trees you could see the large elm tree that stood just inside the cemetery gates from the village far below. After accepting their condolences the carriages left for the mountain plantation and all of the numerous things that waited to be done for the service and gathering that would be sure to follow. Custus was a beloved and well known man all over Greenbrier County and a huge crowd was sure to turn out to see this steward of good will honored and interred. The editor of the paper said many people in the county were calling for the murderers to be caught and summarily executed. On every street corner in Lewisburg small groups of citizens were huddled together talking of the vicious murder.

When the carriages arrived at the mansion they were met by a large crowd of neighbors and friends, both black and white, who had gathered and increased in size ever since the tragic event had taken place. The family was told over and over how sorry every one was about the death of the family patriarch and how glad they were to see them finally arrive. Mabel was glad to see that young Donald Persinger was there and had taken charge of laying out the grave plot and seen to preparing the body for showing. He told her that he and his fiancé Cassie Cutlip had seen to the food preparation as poor Aunt Rose was so distraught she was unable to perform her usual duties as cook and general overseer of the household. After the family was able to eat and rest a short while Mabel made the short walk to the icehouse to see her poor father's remains.

The Reverend Rogers came shortly after they arrived and he spent some time with the family in prayer and discussing plans for the service. He knew this would be by far the largest crowd he had ever preached before and wanted to be sure he did not overlook anything the family might want covered in his eulogy. He personally would have liked to have the service the next day but knew they would want time for people to travel from across the county to pay their respects. Having the large icehouse available made time not as important as it was normally in cases like this and allowed for word to spread and people to travel. On the ride up the mountain road the preacher had taken time to reflect on the tragedy of Mr. McClung's death and of the sudden demise of storeowner Mr. Brown, two real pillars in the Sinking Creek Valley community. He also thought of the tragic death of the young Eggleston couple who had been brutally attacked and murdered by a wolf-dog he had brought home from the war with him. So much tragedy in such a small community in such a short period of time, he thought. The murder of Custus and the act of arson against the Lewis couple had occurred because of the disappearance of a brother of the gang members. I wonder what happened to him, he mused to himself as his mule picked its way carefully up the mountain road. Though he was a man of the cloth and should not allow himself to think that way, he was sure the loss of the brother was not something the average citizen of the valley would care about one way or the other. He let his mind wander. If the missing brother was buried in the new grave on the Lewis place and was murdered, then who killed him, and why? He did not think the Lewis couple had anything to do with the grave but could not decide who would have a reason to kill the person. If the grave did not contain the body of the missing Winslow then who was buried there? If I was going to get rid of a body I would dump it in Roaring Creek when the water was high after a rain. The creek sank just below the village in to a massive opening in the ground called the Sievey Hole. The reverend had visited the place after the creek was high and would never forget the huge hole where the rushing water had eaten a crater in the ground. It was covered with massive trees and boulders that the water had dumped around the opening like they were no more than matchsticks and pebbles. There was a feeling about the place that made one think of another world. This was a world that was populated with prehistoric creatures with three heads and long tails that would whip back and forth toppling everything that crossed their path. A body that went down that hole would disappear forever and never appear in this world again. He felt a shiver down his spine as he thought of the giant opening that was much more than just a hole for water to sink into. Reverend Rogers had once expressed these same thoughts about getting rid of a body with old man Sidney Sammons a some time church goer who had a problem with alcohol. Every few years Sidney would fall off the wagon and usually end up in the Lewisburg jail. He would always go to the big town when his thirst would over ride his righteousness and had spent short periods of time behind bars before. Sidney confided to the preacher that when he was on a drinking spell he felt like someone caught in the currents of Roaring Creek headed uncontrollably toward the Sivvy Hole and was always glad to awake sober in the somehow comforting confines of the county jail. The reverend forced these thoughts out of his mind and concentrated on the prayer that he was offering up for the family of Mr. McClung.

CHAPTER 8

Making Plans

Sheriff James Knight was considerably upset at the case he was now undertaking to solve. Custus McClung had been a friend of his for years and seeing his body laid out in the icehouse had awakened a deep fury in the breast of the lawmen. He had always held Custus in the highest regard and was aware of the good things this active citizen had done for his county and state. The sheriff had been a captain in the 14th Virginia Cavalry and had been wounded severely in the battle of Droop Mountain in November 1863. It had seemed forever for his lung wound to heal and he had suffered greatly over the next year. McClung had been instrumental in getting him on the ballot for sheriff and supported his campaign the previous fall, both with money and political endorsement. The thought of his mentor being gunned down by Northern carpetbagger thugs as he went to the aid of a neighbor's wife made the sheriff deeply angry. He vowed to himself to hunt down his friend's killer.

He had dispatched a deputy to Williamsburg with orders to check with the two doctors there. They were hoping to find if the wounded thug had been taken there for medical treatment since according to Nancy he had been torn up pretty good with Custus's shot gun blast. They rode through Frankford late that night aware that the killers they were looking for may very well live right beside the road and they could be at that time asleep in the living area in the back of the tavern. Sheriff Knight wanted to get a warrant from the judge and make sure every thing was done by the book on this one. He also wanted to get more men together to accompany him back to look for the three Winslow's. The lawmen needed sleep and he decided the next night would do fine for the arrest. He did not think the brothers would be moving anywhere for a while with the one torn up by the shotgun blast and he felt the other two would not leave him in that condition. It was past 4:00 in the morning when they reached Lewisburg and the lawmen fell into their beds exhausted from the day's events.

The sheriff arose at ten o'clock and after dressing and eating breakfast he got together with his chief deputy and they compared notes on the evidence they had been able to gather. They had identification of the dead man by Carl Blake who said he was one of the men who identified himself as a Winslow brother. Melinda at the store also identified him as one of the men who stopped there and threatened the loafers on the store porch. Nancy could identify the Winslow brothers and they had the letter addressed to the Frankford tavern found on the corpse. Knight began filling out the warrant for the arrest of three Winslow's, one of who was Basil Winslow and the first names of the other two were left blank.

Judge Raymond Hailey was a local Greenbrier County gentleman who had supported the Confederate cause in the recent war. Though he was too old to serve in the field, he was known as a firm supporter of the state of Virginia. The lawyers in the area wondered how long he would be allowed to remain on the bench now that the war was over and the Union supporters were in absolute command of the legal system every where else across the state. He had known Custus McClung very well and had been incensed at his senseless murder. He listened intently as Sheriff Knight spelled out his case and he signed the document immediately and set the wheels in motion for the Winslow's arrest. The sheriff quietly notified ten men made up of deputies, constables and Lewisburg city policeman to be ready to ride out at ten o'clock that night from the courthouse lawn. He had decided to arrive very late in the evening hoping the Winslow's would be asleep and unaware of the posse's arrival and their imminent loss of freedom. They all took naps and rested for the anticipated late night raid north to Frankford and rode out at ten twenty p.m.

CHAPTER 9

Arrests, Goodbyes and Burials

Basil Winslow had brooded ever since their excursion to Lewis Mill and he had lost his brother to a shot gun blast. He felt that some one among the Rebel people had killed his brother Bill and in his search for him he had lost another sibling Sammie. The whole incident had gone terribly wrong and now he had his baby brother Ross maybe crippled for life. He paced the floor of the living quarters and drank excessively every day since they had returned. His black mood had not lessened and the two live in barmaids, Abby and Nora tried to keep a safe distance from him. Ross took a lot of dope and whiskey and floated in and out of consciousness. Lawrence stayed in the front of the tavern with the few customers who drifted in and out for a shot of the bust head whiskey he kept in stock. The last two customers left abruptly when Basil came out of the back room about midnight. They took one look at the scowl on the face of the meanest man in town and headed for the door. They had seen Basil when he did not think life was giving him a square shake and didn't wait around to see if this was one of those times.

When they were out of the tavern and up the road out of hearing, one of the slightly inebriated patrons told the other one of the time he saw Basil jump flat footed from the floor and kick Charley Smathers in the chest with both feet. He said he kicked him clear across the fireplace hearth and in to the kindling box and for no reason. Charley always says when Basil is not around that if he could have got him self out of that wood box there would be some sorry looking faces around here. We all know and he does too if he had got out of that wood box Basil Winslow would have killed him. They were so involved in the telling and listening of the wood box tale that they did not see the lawmen until they stepped out of the shadows and demanded silence from them. They identified themselves and asked who was in the tavern. As best the bar patrons could recall there was the three Winslow's and the two bar maids only left in the tavern. As they were discussing this, Lawrence walked by the window to the front door and latched it from within and extinguished five lamps that had kept the barroom interior visible from the street. The front of the tavern was in darkness with a dim light shining back in the living quarters. Sheriff Knight said they would give them an hour or so and let sleep over come them before barging in. While waiting the lawmen opened a sack they had brought holding three 16lb. sledgehammers and waited. After nearly an hour had passed they quietly slipped to each of the three doors, two or three together. On a prearranged count, they at almost the exact time brought the heavy hammers with a roundhouse swing into the door locks right at the latch. The three doors exploded in a rush of crushed metal and splintered wood. Screams of terror and curses came from inside the house and the deputies stepped inside the door openings and hurled the heavy hammers into the house breaking tables, chairs or walls in a crash that brought forth more screams from the frightened women. Behind them stepped more lawmen with lit lanterns held high in one hand and cocked pistols in their gun hand. Abby and Nora ran naked and screaming from the first bedroom, their ample breasts bobbing in the lamplight. Right behind them Basil came out with a Colt pistol in his hand, he fired and the slug slammed in to the door facing. Sheriff Knight hit him across the face with the side of his heavy Le Matt revolver. He crumpled to the floor like a sack of feed.

Lawrence was captured and bound before he ever got completely awake. He howled in protest and bucked up and down but to no avail. Three of the deputies threatened to bust his head open and he calmed down. Ross was in the same large room with Lawrence and despite the gunshot and screaming never even woke up. The posse had brought a large farm wagon and they checked the unconscious Ross for arms and finding none carried him, mattress and all, to the wagon and laid him in the back. They tied his hands and feet loosely together and dumped his hogtied brothers in the opposite end of the wagon bed. In five minutes the three suspects were on their way down the Seneca Trail toward the Lewisburg jail. Making sure the two naked barmaids were not hurt the caravan was in motion quickly. The only concession to comfort the lawbreakers were given was a pillow propped under the sleeping Ross's gun shot foot for elevation.

In less than three hours the brothers were in the county jail. A doctor was sent for to check out the now bleeding leg of Ross and he was taken to a hospital where he could be treated. Two heavily armed guards were dispatched out side the door and window of his room. He slept through out the whole arrest and wagon trip to Lewisburg and continued to sleep at the hospital. Back at the jail Basil was in full force, screaming for a lawyer and bondsmen to get him out. He was treated to a slamming steel door and largely ignored until morning. Lawrence sat in silence and stared at Basil, as if saying, how did we get to this lowly state of existence?

The next morning Judge Hailey decided that the risk of the men running if given bond would be too great to chance. Ross was allowed to stay at the hospital under guard until he could be safely removed. The doctors said this could be some time because of the extent of his wounds. Basil screamed all morning for a lawyer and finally one was found who agreed to talk with him. When the lawyer exited the jail he was seen going straight to the telegraph office. In no time at all he was back at the jail with a message for Basil. Sit tight, help is on the way, the message said.

"Don't worry we will be out of here in no time." Basil said to a somber Lawrence.

The lawyer Hudson agreed to represent him and he sent his associate up to Frankford with a message to the two saloon girls. It contained a list of items that Basil needed including a change of clothes for him and his two brothers. Also, on the list was a boot box that was hidden under a loose board under Basil's bed. The lawyer's assistant retrieved the box, could not resist taking a peek inside and spied a considerable amount of cash and other papers. He admonished the two saloon girls, who fit the new term for loose women to a t, to keep the saloon closed and allow no one into the back living quarters. They could stay there until he got out of jail but they damn well better never have any one else there. The new term was hooker. This was given to the drove of prostitutes that followed General Hookers Union army in Virginia during the war. Basil had the lawyer's man tell them he would be watching them and if they disobeyed his orders they would be eternally sorry. The girls seemed too frightened by Winslow's threats to disobey him in the least it seemed to the law assistant. He left them there promising strict obedience to his instructions and returned with the box and clothes to Lewisburg.

The next morning Judge Hailey had the two Winslow's that could walk appear before him in court. He set their trial date for two weeks and five days from that date. Lawyer Hudson appeared with them and said he would be representing the brothers in court. The district attorney charged them with murder, arson and assault on the woman whose house was burned. Judge Hailey officially denied bail for the Winslow's and ordered them held until the trial date.

The monotony of the jail life had the high strung Basil walking a tightrope. He felt like he would explode at any time and paced the cell back and forth, back and forth. His attorney was able to keep him in cigars and Lawrence in chewing tobacco but every thing passed to the prisoners was checked carefully by the jails deputies before it was allowed in to them. After three and one half days he finally quit pacing and lay down on the thin mattress and slept awhile. When he woke up he noticed an older man dressed like a farmer snoring in the cell next to him. Lawrence said he had been brought in drunk while Basil slept. He said the man was from up Lewis Mill way and when he woke up they should see if he could tell them anything about Bill. The man slept all that afternoon and night he held his head in his hands the next morning and moaned pitifully every few seconds. It was so irritating Basil had to struggle to keep from screaming at him to just shut up. Lawrence had tried to convince his brother that if they could make friends with this fellow he might be able to give them some information that would help them find out what happened to Bill. Lawrence had by far the most engaging way about him and they decided he would be the one to cozy up to the old fellow. They knew if he was in for only being drunk in public he would be getting out soon maybe even that same day. When their breakfast of boiled eggs, fatty bacon and strong black coffee was brought in Lawrence felt the time was right. He waited until the man drank all of his coffee and walked to the bars and said,

"Here, you look like you could use this more than me."

He handed his cup through to the grateful prisoner and he gulped it hurriedly even though it was still quite hot. The older man thanked him profusely and when asked offered up his name as Sydney Sammons from up near Cold Knob. Lawrence engaged him in conversation enough to loosen him up. He could not give them any real information about their missing brother, however. He just could not recall ever seeing anyone who matched their description. In response to their questions about the Lewis couple who lived in the holler up Roaring Creek, he said that Clarke Lewis absolutely was a man to be believed. He had been away in the army and came home for just a short time and then went to Monroe County and married that pretty young girl and brought her to Lewis Mill to make a home with him. He assured them that she had never been there before he married her.

Lawrence asked if he knew there was a fresh grave in the holler on a knoll above the house. He answered that he did not, in such a forthright way that even these life time doubters had to believe he was speaking the truth. Basil asked the poor hung over member of Reverend Roger's church, if he was going to get rid of a body near Lewis Mill. What would he do with it? As he asked the question, Basil leaned way forward toward the other prisoner as if he was hanging on his every word.

"Well sir, I ain't got no reason to get rid of a body, but if I did I'd just throw it down the Sievey Hole."

"What the hell is a Sievey hole?" Basil asked in a surprisingly calm and conspiratorial tone of voice.

"Well, it's the sinks of the crick. It's where Roaring Crick goes in to the ground down below the Mill. When that cricks high it just boils down into that hole and where it comes back up at two or three different places the openings ain't big enough for a body to ever rise up again. Why, don't you see it'd be gone forever."

"Who, beside you, knows about this place?" Basil asked, his voice was just a little threatening this time but still pleasant enough for conversation.

"Why, most everybody knows that crick sinks down there, not everybody has been down there, but they know it sure enough sinks and then rises again on down the valley. It ain't no secret at all. A person wouldn't have to tote a body all the way down there though. If the crick is up at all you could just toss it in and let the current do the toting for you."

"Where did they get a name like that? What does it mean?" asked Lawrence.

"I think it comes from a sieve, like you drain things through and let liquid go through but not the big things. Like trees and huge rocks can't get through just things of a certain size. A mans body would double up and go right down it but a big limb might get crossways and still be there when the crick goes back down." said Sidney.

Basil leaned back and winked at Lawrence then asked Sammons if he knew a man named Custus McClung that lived up that way.

"Sure I do, everybody knows Mr. McClung, he's one of the nicest people you've ever met. He'd help anybody, anytime. How do you know Custus? He asked warily.

"Well, Mr. Sammons, I know him because I killed him. Yes, sir I shot him right in the chest just the other day. That's why we are here in this jail." Basil rocked back and began laughing in a maniacal tone. His head tilted back and he laughed and laughed as he gazed at the dirty ceiling.

Sammons began screaming at the top of his lungs for someone to come get him out. He yelled so loud the jailer thought he was dying and rushed from the front area towards his cell. "Murderer, murderer, murderer," he screamed as Basil laughed louder and tears streamed down his cheeks.

"Get me out of here now," demanded Sammons. "I 'm only in here cause I got drunk. These men killed Custus McClung. Now, let me out I tell you, let me out, now."

The jailer really had no reason to hold Sammons any longer and the racket he was raising soon got old. He turned the lock in the cell door and the old man nearly knocked him over running to the front of the building and out the front door. He had been drunk in Lewisburg since the day before the shootings and had no idea Mr. McClung was dead. The insane laughter followed him out the door. He entered the sheriff's office next door in a run. Sheriff Knight listened to him tell the story about the prisoner's that had been in the next cell. After he finished it was his turn to listen to the sheriff relate the events that happened in the holler on Roaring Creek. Sammons was told by the sheriff to keep the details of the conversation with Basil and Lawrence fresh in his mind because he may be called to testify in the upcoming trial. He had calmed down somewhat and was now sober, he started for his home in Lewis Mill. He wanted to reach there in order to attend whatever services they may be planning for Mr. McClung. He hoped he would be able to attend the funeral at least.

The Winslow's lawyer Hudson came to the jail right after Sammons had fled. Basil was still laughing like a mad man until he saw his attorney standing outside his bars looking at him with a quizzical look on his face.

"Get me out of here, Hudson." He said with a sudden scowl. "I've got to find my brother Bill, I know those Rebs did him in some how. Did you bring my belongings like I told you?"

"Yes, my man made the trip and passed your message on to the two women. He said they were too afraid of you to do anything but what you wanted from them. The jailer will let you have the clothes but nothing else. I went through the box and ," he lowered his voice somewhat, "There was five deeds to property and seventy two thousand dollars in United States money in the box. I have it locked in a safe in my office for you. No one else knows of what was in the box, not even my man whom I trust completely. "

"Well I would not go trusting him too much cause there's about $28,000.00 dollars missing from the box if what you say it contained is correct. That box should have had $100,000.00 dollars in it. No one knew that box was there except my brother Bill. My other brothers did not know of its existence. Now, by God, either your man or you skimmed money from me and I won't stand for it."

"My dear Mr. Winslow I can assure neither myself nor my assistant took a dime from your box of belongings. If my man Tetterton brought me a box containing a certain amount, then that is what was in the box. He has been with me for more than twenty years and I will say again I would trust him with my life. I am a reputable loyal Unionist and you know this. You have the telegram from Wheeling vouching for my reliability from Judge Cockrell. He and I go back a long way and I can assure you the judge does not treat recommendations lightly. Perhaps, and I tread lightly here, your missing brother Bill was in the process of a business deal you were not aware of when unfortunate circumstances prevailed on him. Could it be that

Bill had availed himself of some of your funds in order to make some really good investment that he intended to surprise you with later? It does happen, Mr. Winslow, every day actually." Hudson said in the most casual and non threatening tone he could muster.

"I will have to think about this, Hudson. I had not checked the box for some time before Bill came up missing. For your sake and your assistants I hope that after pondering on this, I come to that conclusion. You must know by now that I am the kind of man who deep down just don't give a shit. Some one is going to answer some questions as to what happened to Brother Bill. There's going to be more people dead than the fat man with the shot gun in the buggy when I get out of here.

"Here, now though I am your lawyer and sworn to secrecy about our conversations you should not express those sentiments around others. I implore you sir," said Hudson quickly and firmly.

"I just want to make sure you know where I stand," hissed Basil. "Now represent us and get us out of here."

"This judge will not let you out on bail, no matter how much we offer to put up. I can not get you out until you are found innocent at the trial," said Hudson and he turned and walked out of the cell area of the jail.

Basil seemed unaware of the possibility that he and his brothers could be convicted of murder. He was already thinking about making a trip to check out the grave in the holler and perhaps to the infamous Seivy Hole. He not only wanted to find out where Bill was now the missing money was also a catalyst for finding him. He thought about the situation and decided that Bill must have been ape shit crazy in love with some mountain girl. He did not think Bill would have a business deal working with out his knowledge. Bill was not the sort for surprises, more likely he had taken what he considered his share of the money and intended to use it in some fashion with his new love. Perhaps the money had led to his demise what ever it turned out to be and not the jealous husband angle at all. We will take care of this after the trial, when we get out, he confided to Lawrence. He was determined to handle the pressure of doing jail time and forced himself to relax. Hudson kept telling him when he would come to talk about his defense that he had an ace in the hole. He went over and over what happened that day and seemed to have both brothers on the same page. The important thing he told Basil was to relax and not bring attention to himself and above all not to threaten any one else.

Donald Persinger had been on the mountain at Twin Sugars for two days now helping any way he could to make it easy on the McClung family. He traveled back to his parent's house to get his only suit, a plain black coat and trousers that he had before the war. As he passed the Eggleston lane he turned up it to pick a few of the Golden Delicious apples that grew in abundance in the trees below the house.

He had spied a bucket near the back door that was rusted out to much to hold water but would do just fine holding a few of the wonderful apples his daddy loved so much. He glanced at the well apron and saw an iron setting there on the wooden board. He picked it up and got the idea that the iron would make a thoughtful gift for his fiance' Cassie. As he held it in his hand he had the sudden idea of painting the iron with a scene he had seen in a painting of the Bahamas. Palm trees and clear blue water with pure white sand that glistened in the sunlight. That was what he would do with this iron. He discovered he had an aptitude for painting scenes when he was in the army. During some of the long weeks of inactivity the soldiers would sometimes do things that were new to them to pass the time. Some whittled things and made knickknacks, one soldier carved beautiful ducks that looked so real one would have to walk lightly to keep them from taking to flight. Donald had tried his hand at painting and was surprised to find he could paint some amazingly life like scenes with out a lot of trouble. This would be a wedding gift for Cassie and she could keep it on their mantle or on a cupboard beside the table. He also thought of the good deed he was doing for the iron, rescuing it from a life of rust and neglect if left outside and the constant strain of repeated heating and if brought inside for someone to labor with. He eagerly placed the iron in the pocket of his jacket. He carried the apples to his mother who cooked them that evening for supper along with big cathead biscuits covered in butter. He left the iron in his cave bed room and decided he would start the painting of it as soon as every thing at the McClung house hold was under control. He balanced the iron in his hand and thought about the scene he would paint on it. He knew that Cassie would be very excited to receive a thing of labor that she could look at and not have to use. She had shown him her hope chest full of things to use after her marriage and she had an iron already. This one, he grinned to himself, will be to look at only.

The funeral service for Custus McClung was the largest gathering the log church at Lewis Mill had ever seen. His body lay in state for one hour before the service began and a huge crowd had already gathered before the body even arrived from the plantation on the mountain. Farmers, plain mountain folks, black folks, and rich politicians all descended on the log church. Judges, lawyers, lawmen, distant relatives and close relatives were there, even casual acquaintances were all there to pay their respects to this greatly loved citizen. His passing would have always drawn a crowd but the barbaric way his parting was accomplished seemed to bring out everyone in the county. The field across the road was crammed with every kind of horse or mule drawn conveyance. The lucky ones got there first and availed themselves of the shade under the locust trees. The late comers left their wagons and animals wherever they could find a spot, in the shade or in the sun. No one took a chance of missing this grand send off service Reverend Rogers had planned for Mr. McClung.

The text he had chosen brought tears to the eyes of most of the audience at once. After the hymn, Let it Be opened the service he led them in prayer. Another hymn followed, No Tears in Heaven. Then the preacher read the text, Greater love hath no man than that he lay down his life for his friend. What a fitting passage for the situation, for no doubt it was Custus going to

Nancy's aid that led him to his early grave. Every window was open and jammed with heads trying to see and hear the reverends sermon. The double pine doors were both propped open and the crowd was standing shoulder to shoulder to hear the soothing words. Not an eye was dry, as the preacher told of what happened that day, when the bad men had come to the peaceful valley to find one of their missing own and would not take no for an answer. He spoke of the arrested men waiting trial in the county jail. They were awaiting the judgment for their crimes, the crime of murder against the good man lying here. Then he spoke of the judgment we all had waiting and preached for nearly an hour of the time when we all would have to lay down our lives. Were we ready for that? He asked. Were we ready to answer the call to judgment here or in the life to come? He said that Mr. McClung had answered his call and called for everyone there to be ready for the time that their call came. Then he started singing in a smooth baritone voice the old hymn When he calls me I will answer. He closed the service with a strong plaintive prayer asking for the lord to accept poor Mr. McClung's soul in to paradise and to comfort his daughter and his whole family. He said, the service was concluded there and would continue at the McClung home cemetery on Twin Sugars Mountain.

Chapter 10
Sorrow and Happiness

Most of the audience was attending the burial service and the procession stretched out for over a mile up the mountain road. Not since the cavalry from the Jones-Imboden raid in the spring of 1863 passed through had such a procession been seen in the valley. That procession of 5,000 troops, followed by hundreds of horses, cattle and captured stores had taken hours to pass through the village. That had been a celebration that lasted for hours. This was one long group of mourners with heavy hearts the normal feeling. Some were already thinking of exacting revenge on the carpetbaggers who had killed their most popular citizen.

When they reached the top of the mountain and gathered around the family cemetery the village with its log church could be seen far below them in the valley. The long view Custus had enjoyed every day of his life was still there for the seeing. Death had taken away the vision from his eyes but his spirit could enjoy the view forever. More prayer followed and his body was committed to the earth. Everyone kind of drifted toward the veranda and the huge sugar maples that surrounded it. Donald Persinger and Cassie Cutlip had, with all the inhabitants of the plantation set out huge wooden tables loaded with all different kind of delicious food for the mourners. A few politicians spoke on Custus's life and some eulogized him. All agreed on what a wonderful citizen he had always been. Various locals rose to tell of the kind things he had done for them down through the years. Carr spoke of him taking care of his farm while he was gone to the war. Clarke followed with his thanks for the things he had done for him over the years, both before, during and after the war. His voice broke as he told of Custus coming so unhesitating to Nancy's aid that day. Both of them felt he had undoubtedly saved her life that day at the cost of his own.

One of the well dressed politicians that had come from Lewisburg said they had the three Winslow's in jail there and a trial date had been set for the seventeenth of the month. Restless murmurings came from the crowd when the mention of a trial was spoken. Many of the associates of the law urged them to be patient and let the law work through its channels. He said that they were sure to be found guilty and hung. The mutterings continued and the lawmen let the subject alone and many began eating the good food laid out before them. After an hour or two many in the crowd began expressing their regrets to Mabel and the family and making their way off the mountain, especially the ones who had come from Lewisburg and various other places in the county that were just as far away.

Mabel asked Clarke, Nancy, Carr and Melinda to stay awhile after most of the others had gone. She and her husband John Morgan wanted to ask their opinion on something. Mabel said she and John would like to stay on the mountain until September and then they felt they would have to return to Covington, to his law practice and to enroll the children in the fall and winter classes at their schools. She said they needed someone to run the plantation for them, some one to move into the mansion and work the fields, crops and livestock and keep the place going. They would pay them a supervisor's salary and all their food, clothes and rent for the mansion would be furnished along with the salary. The Morgan's would visit the plantation around Christmas time and perhaps a few weeks in the summer, otherwise the supervisor would have full and complete access to the mansion. Her father had always been very fond of Clarke she said and she knew he would be the first one he would want her to offer the position. She also knew he and Nancy would need a place to live with the burning of their home so recently. Mabel could tell the couple was startled by her offer and quickly assured them they could take some time to think about it and let her know later. She again said she and Morgan would not be leaving the mountain for at least two months and they did not have to make their decision now. They thanked her for the offer and said they would let her know as soon as they could.

As they went down the mountain Clarke spoke to Nancy of their dilemma. She said they could look at the place in the holler as good, Carr's place as better, and the place on the mountain as best or they could reverse that order and she would be just as happy. Clarke thought of how lucky he had been to find her. She was so down to earth and realistic, he knew she could be just as happy in a rebuilt cabin in the holler as she would be in the grand mansion called Twin Sugars. That was just one of the many, many things he loved about his new bride. He suggested to her that perhaps they could stop and spend the night alone together in Carr's house. She eagerly agreed and he pulled the wagon into the house's lane. He yelled back at Carr that they were going to stay on the mountain in his house that evening and would see them the next day.

Carr had not had the opportunity to be alone with Melinda since he had left for Covington the day of the incident at the holler property. Just below his house was a place where the wagon road made a loop to the left before rejoining the main road a quarter mile below. He pulled the buggy they were riding over and took the loop off the main road and stopped at a beautiful overlook that had been created by the cutting of timber the year before. He looked into her green eyes and told her she knew how much he cared for her. His hand lifted the ring from his side pocket and he asked if she would like to spend the rest of their lives together. Tears sprang to her eyes and she answered that indeed she would like that. Yes, yes, yes she cried as he slipped the ring on her finger. The horse paced up and down in its traces and he quickly set the brake on the buggy. He had been so immersed in his proposal that he had forgotten all about it. They embraced and their mouths met in a long and passionate kiss that left her breathless. She seemed so happy and that of course in turn made him happy. They were two mature adults who had both seen heartache and tragedy in their lives but they were giggling and gushing like teenagers as they watched the sun set in the west as they lay on a quilt he had spread on the mossy ground beside a huge oak stump. They made plans and talked of the future as the horse picked its way down the mountain road in the darkness. When he let her out in front of her Aunt Margie's house an hour after full darkness had descended on the valley, he told her she had made him the happiest man in the new state of West Virginia. She ran up the steps and into the house and he could hear her calling out, "Aunt Margie, Aunt Margie."

CHAPTER 11

Pre Trial

Per Basil Winslow's instructions his brother Sammie was buried in the cemetery north of town with the remains of the Northern troops that died in the battle of Lewisburg. The sheriff did not think much of placing Sammie's remains with the bodies of the brave Ohio soldiers who had charged the Confederate cannons that May morning in 1862, but he allowed it to proceed. No one was there at the burial other than a Baptist minister who said a few words, the undertaker, his assistant and the two hookers from Frankford. In a strange twist of fate all of the Yankee troop's bodies including Sammie's were disinterred and shipped to the new cemetery at Staunton and buried there three years later. Thus, Sammie Winslow, deserter from the battlefield at Monocacy, killer of a fellow soldier who he knifed to death in an alley and dumped naked into the Ohio River and murderer of Custus McClung was interred with a hero's honor in the national cemetery. His body had the gun salute and all the pomp and ceremony performed over it that the real hero's remains received.

The prosecuting attorney for Greenbrier County was Mike Kelly. He had been elected in 1864 running on the Democratic ticket. He had served two years in the Confederate army and been wounded at Droop Mountain. A musket ball had shattered his kneecap and he still walked with a limp and sometimes a cane a year and a half later. He had never prosecuted a case with the victim being such a well known individual and wanted to be sure he left nothing to chance. He traveled to Lewis Mill and interviewed every one he could find who had any thing at all to do with the case. Nancy, Clarke, Melinda, Carl Blake, the three store front loafers, Mason McClung and another of Custus's former slaves named Shop of the Twin Sugars plantation. Sidney Sammons who had been in the city jail with Basil and Lawrence would also be called to testify as to Basil's laughter filled, bragging confession to the McClung murder.

He traveled to the holler to see the murder scene and was walked through the scenario by a strong and resolute Nancy with Clarke beside her. She gave him all the details and he told her to be just like that on the witness stand and they would see justice done. He spent three nights at the hotel in Lewis Mill and was satisfied when he left that he had a strong, virtually iron clad case against the three brothers. He arrived back in Lewisburg and worked every day up until the trial on the case and planned how the evidence would be presented. He felt he had enough witnesses to place the Winslow's at the place in the holler on that day and Nancy as an eyewitness to the actual murder. He still would have liked to have known who was buried in the grave on the knoll in the holler. Kelly did not think it had anything to do with his case but he was sure the lawyer Hudson would bring it up in front of the jury. If Hudson could insinuate the grave held the body of Bill Winslow then he might be able to shift the burden of guilt toward Nancy and Clarke and away from his client. He would try to make it look like they were guilty of something and that would be a basis for the groundwork that Nancy may be lying and that Custus fired first making the killing a case of self defense, thus, freeing the Winslow's. It was a long shot he knew but it was the only tactic he could think of that the seasoned attorney Hudson could possibly have to use in the defense of the obviously guilty brothers.

Two days before the trial a tall thin grey haired man with dark piercing eyes and dark clothing arrived in a black buggy. He was accompanied by a very tall, well dressed man, about thirty five years old who looked like he might be the older man's protector. They parked the buggy at the front of the courthouse columns and inquired to the judge's chambers. Judge Raymond Hailey looked up to see the two enter his office without so much as a knock. To his inquiry of can I help you? The older one replied that he was Judge Malcolm Holmes from Wheeling and he had traveled a long way and wished to address Judge Raymond Hailey.

"I'm Judge Raymond Hailey. How may I help you Judge Holmes."

"I was sent here by the governor, Your Honor, to preside over the trial of the three Winslow brothers from Wheeling."

"I'm the judge of this district sir and as such, I plan to preside over the up coming trial that is scheduled to commence in two days hence," Said Judge Hailey.

The newly arrived judge handed over a letter signed by the governor ordering him to give up his seat on the bench to Judge Holmes for the trial of the Winslow's only. The letter said Judge Holmes had full authority in the upcoming trial and was not to be interfered with in any way and was to be helped if requested. The man with the judge was Masterson from the state attorney general's office. He was not only there to protect Holmes, he was also there to enforce the letters instructions. Judge Hailey was instructed to retire to his home until the trial was finished and turn over the key to his office and any papers or needed item.

"Why, may I ask is this being done and why is the governor and attorney generals office involved in a county matter?" asked Judge Hailey. "I think I deserve to know why I am being removed from this case."

"Of course, you can be told the reason," said Holmes, "there is more than one reason though, first, you were close to the murdered man and may not be able to maintain impartiality in the courtroom. Second, these accused men are well known in the financial circles of Wheeling, important men are interested in their welfare. The third reason is this area was a hot bed of secessionist scoundrels who can not be trusted to provide a fair proceeding for the loyal Union men who are going to be on trial for their lives. Consider this a blessing Hailey, I preside at the trial and they can never say that you swayed the verdict one way or the other. After the trial we will leave your fair town and you will be back on the bench just like before. Now make your self scarce for a few short days and I will handle this problem. Where can a man get a good steak in this town?"

Judge Hailey was already gone out the door, he made a stop at the telegraph office and sent a confirmation to his contact in Wheeling, waited for the answer and rode his buggy out to his home on the southern edge of town. He would spend the next few days reading and stewing at the idea that the trial of Custus's murderers would be handled by a Union judge who was a ringer sent in by the swindlers from Wheeling to steer the Winslow's toward freedom.

As soon as Judge Hailey was out of sight, Holmes sent Masterson for Hudson the lawyer representing the Winslow brothers. When he arrived, though he had been notified by letter that a change of judges was happening, he had never met Judge Holmes. This was Friday morning and the trial was scheduled to start Monday with jury selection being the first thing on the agenda. Hudson was surprised when he was informed there would be no jury at the trial. The sitting judge would try the case himself and make the determination of guilt or innocence and sentence if a guilty verdict was reached. Not much chance of guilty being the verdict was the feeling Hudson got from the judge who would preside at the trial. The accused had the option of going without a jury but the lawyer knew of no capital murder case being tried that way in his thirty years of practice in the Greenbrier area. They would take no chance of a secessionist sympathizing jury drawn from the local citizens finding the accused guilty. Judge and defense lawyer proceeded to plan the strategy for the direction the trial would take. The district attorney was unaware that the deck was stacked against him before the trial even started.

Chapter 12

The Wedding and the Serenade

That Saturday of the weekend before the trial was the date set for the wedding of Donald Persinger and Cassie Cutlip. They decided to have an outside wedding at The Blue Hole, a popular swimming spot on Roaring Creek that ran beside the cave home of his parents. Luckily, Mother Nature cooperated and the afternoon wedding was held beneath a clear blue sky that lovely July day. Above the deep blue waters of the swimming hole was a cascading waterfall that was far enough away to make the preachers words audible and still frame the wedding party in the beauty of the falling waters.

Many of the neighbors came from the surrounding hills and valleys. Cassie and her mother and sisters wore beautiful corsages made of the blooming rhododendrons gathered from the banks and hillsides. Clarke, Nancy, Carr, Melinda, Margie, John and Mabel Morgan and children, Aunt Rose, Mason and several others from Twin Sugars were there. After the ceremony everyone went up the road to the Cutlip residence for a celebration that lasted in to the night. Tables of food were spread under the trees in front of the house. Later, a Mr. Woods broke out his fiddle and he was soon joined by a guitar and banjo player. Jars of homemade whiskey were discreetly passed around adding to the merriment. A level spot of the front yard was used for dancing and Woods began calling figures for a square dance. Most every one, young and old danced a jig at one time or the other that evening.

Donald presented his bride with the iron he had rescued from the rust. He had painted a lovely tropical beach scene just like he had imagined when he found it. She was very happy to receive it and expressed surprise at his painting talent. She had known nothing of his new found skill and could not believe he had painted it himself just for her. They agreed that after looking at it for awhile one could almost hear the roar of the ocean and see the palm trees sway in the tropical breeze. When the snow was piling up in the winter and the cold wind was howling through the mountains they could look at it together and imagine they were there. Everyone marveled at the delightful gift young Persinger had made for his beautiful new bride out of a discarded iron.

The next day, Sunday a large group of wagons and buggy's made their way down the valley to Lewisburg for the long awaited trial. They all could not wait to see the murderers receive their just and righteous sentence that every one of them felt should be death by hanging. Many of them took provisions for camping out as they were certain that the hotels and boarding houses would be filled with trial spectators. The Morgan's had sent one of their workers weeks before with money to secure a reservation at the General Lewis Inn. Their three children were being cared for by Aunt Rose back on the mountain. Carr, Melinda, Nancy and Clarke planned to stay with the brother's cousin who had a large home near the courthouse.

Late that night they all met at the district attorneys office. He went over with each one the questions he would ask them and told them what he expected the defense lawyer would also ask them. He seemed satisfied with the plan he had devised and the order in which they would be called. He told them not to be nervous and tell the truth in all instances. If they were not sure whether they had responded enough to a question, he instructed them to look at him. When he looked down at the floor that was to signal a yes or continue talking but if he looked to the right that meant not to elaborate or stop talking. He went through scenarios to show them what he meant. All responded that they understood. He told them they were there to bolster the state's case against the Winslow's. He asked them if they personally thought the Winslow's had killed Mr. McClung with out provocation. They all nodded yes. Kelly then told them that tomorrow they would convince the jury that their friend and neighbor had been murdered trying to help one of them out of a bad situation. The meeting was adjourned and everyone went to get some rest for the administering of justice the next day.

Chapter 13
The Trial

The bailiff called the court to order the next morning at 9:00 sharp.

"All rise for the Honorable Judge Malcolm Holmes."

Everyone in the packed courtroom except the Winslow's and their attorney were surprised when the tall, silver haired, Holmes walked to the judge's chair and sat down instead of the portly Judge Hailey. Mutterings were heard from the crowd and Holmes worked the gavel. He proceeded to inform them that the case of the State of West Virginia vs. Basil, Lawrence and Ross Winslow was now open. They had been charged with the murder of Custus McClung, the arson of a home owned by Clarke Lewis and forceful restraint of one Nancy Lewis on June, 7, 1865. He further informed the court that the accused brothers had chosen to waive a jury trial and would be tried before the bench. In other words he, the judge would determine their guilt or innocence and pronounce sentence if a guilty verdict was rendered. The surprise was evident to all by the gasps and immediate murmuring that started as soon as the judge made that announcement. Kelly, the prosecuting attorney was blind sided by both of these turn of events. Judge

Holmes said that any one who had been called for jury duty could be excused since there would be no jury. Only two of the more than thirty potential jurors chose to give up their chairs and depart the courtroom.

"We will now begin our opening arguments. Mr. Kelly as the prosecutor for the state you will be first to proceed," said Judge Holmes.

Mike Kelly still stunned by the dismissal of the jurors arose from his seat and began his summation.

"Your honor we are here today to present our case against these three men for the murder of one of the greatest citizens Greenbrier County had ever known."

"Objection," said Hudson. "Your honor, we are not here to praise the status of the victim in this case. One man's live can not be seen as superior over any other in a court of law."

"Sustained, Mr. Prosecutor, refrain from praising the deceased," said Judge Holmes.

Kelly rolled his eyes and looked briefly at the ceiling, he knew this was going to be an uphill battle all the way with this strange and unusual change that had been thrust up on the trial.

"Very well, your honor, the state will prove that on June, 7 of this year. These three defendants went on a mission to the northern end of Greenbrier County at Lewis Mill to find their lost brother. They stopped at the general store there and inquired very forcefully of three gentlemen taking the sun on the front porch, if they had seen the missing brother. When told they had not, these men, the three Winslow brothers proceeded to verbally abuse the local citizens relaxing in the morning sun. Where upon, one Melinda Nelson, being the store manager, asked them to leave the premises. They did so after again verbally abusing her and the three locals and proceeded north up the Cold Knob road.

They next encountered Mr. Carl Blake on the road and proceeded to beat him severely with a coiled rope about the head and face. Mr. Blake sought shelter after they left him, by the side of a rushing mountain stream that ran beside the road. After leaving him there, beaten and bloody, the three proceeded to the home of Mr. Clarke Lewis, since Mr. Lewis was not home at that time they started to aggressively throw outlandish accusations upon his poor defenseless wife. We will prove that Basil Winslow demanded that the others burn the house and physically forced Mrs. Lewis to the out side of the burning house. We will also prove, your honor, that Custus McClung seeing the smoke from his house high above came to help Mrs. Lewis. He was cold bloodedly shot to death by all three of the Winslow's. Mr. McClung was able to return fire before he was killed and managed to shoot Sammie Winslow to death and wound the defendant Ross Winslow. We submit that the only thing that kept Mrs. Lewis from being harmed further was the appearance of Custus McClung, her good and generous neighbor to her rescue. He paid for it with his life when he came upon this cold and murderous gang of armed roughs. We will prove that the men were seen riding from the scene with Ross Winslow wounded by Custus McClung clinging to his bloody horse. We will introduce the gentlemen who had his buggy strong armed from him by the defendants and hear the testimony of the doctor who treated Ross Winslow's wounds that same day in his office in Williamsburg. We can and will prove that these three defendants did commit murder, arson and assault that day June 7, 1865."

Kelly had deliberately left out the witness Sidney Sammons, who would testify that Basil Winslow had admitted and even bragged about committing the murder.

"The defense will now present their argument to the court," Judge Holmes announced.

Walt Hudson, the defendants lawyer began his opening statement, he said he would prove that the Winslow's had indeed gone to Lewis Mill to look for their missing brother that day and had been involved in the gun battle. They would present evidence that proved the whole thing was provoked by McClung and even Mrs. Lewis. He warned that things would come out in this trial that may offend sensitive ears. He hinted that clandestine goings on had been the root of an incident that escalated out of hand by, not the Winslow's, but others who would be called to the witness stand during the course of the trial. He thanked the court and returned to his chair beside Basil, who was exhibiting a surprisingly calm demeanor.

The first witness Kelly called was one of the three locals who were tongue lashed by Basil at the store that morning. He said they tried to convince the Winslow's that it would be hard to find a lady fitting the description they gave of the woman whose husband was away in the war. He said they told him four women up the road matched that description but on reflecting on it later he personally knew of no less than seven women who had men away in the war. The only thing Hudson asked him on cross examination was had he ever been in the holler where the shooting had taken place. When the witness answered yes he had. He then asked him if he had been there in the last six months and the witness answered negatively.

The district attorney next called Carl Blake to the stand. He told of the beating he suffered at the hands of Basil Winslow that morning. He said that he did not know why Basil had so suddenly and viciously began whipping him across the head and face with the rope. Basil glared at the witness in a threatening way the entire time he was on the witness stand. The look was a withering scowl that had not been seen on the defendants face in the courtroom and went away when Blake was dismissed by Hunter and he left the stand. There seemed to be something in Blake's kind and open expression that brought out the meanest and most debased behavior in Basil Winslow. Blake told the court of lying on the bank by the creek and seeing the three defendants pass back down the road with Ross bleeding badly from his leg below the knee. The side of his horse was wet with blood from the wounds. Hudson asked when it was his turn, if he had ever been in the holler where the shootings had occurred? "Of course," he answered, many, many times.

"Have you seen the fresh grave there on the knoll?"

"Yes, I have seen the grave." Carl replied.

The third question was did he know who was buried in that grave.

"No, no I don't know who is in that grave", said Carl.

"No further questions, your Honor," said Hudson.

Next called as a witness was Melinda Nelson, she walked to the stand and took the oath like the other witnesses before her. She was asked where she worked and what her position was at the store. She answered she was the manager. Then she was asked if she had ever seen the defendants before and if so where and under what circumstances. She said they had stopped at the store that morning in June and were asking for information about the whereabouts of their missing brother. She revealed that they had gotten angry and abusive toward her and the three men who were on the store porch that morning. She revealed that she asked them to leave and they had cursed her. She then corrected herself that it was not them who had verbally abused her, only the one and pointed at Basil. She said the rest of the riders had not spoken at all while they were at the store, at least not that she had heard. On cross examination the defense lawyer Hudson asked her three questions. Had she ever been to the property where the shooting occurred?

"Yes," she answered.

"Have you ever seen a fresh grave there?"

"Yes," she answered.

The third question was did she know who was buried in that grave.

"No, I do not know," was her answer.

Up next was the man who had his buggy taken by force and intimidation by the brothers. When asked if the men who took his horse and buggy and left him stranded were in the courtroom and he pointed at the Winslow brothers. He was asked how many men were present that morning? He replied there were three. Was one of the men injured? Yes, that one, he said pointing at Ross who sat at the defense table with his injured foot propped up in a chair. The defense attorney said he had no questions for the witness and he was excused.

Holmes called for a one hour break for lunch and every one exited the courtroom to answer the call of nature and satisfy the rumbling emptiness of their stomach. Carr, Clarke and their two ladies walked the short block down to the Fort Savannah Inn and all four ordered the pot roast. Over lunch they discussed the switch in judges and wondered what it meant. The fact that the defendants did not want a jury trial was not lost on them. They all four agreed that the judge was probably there to help the Winslow's escape the gallows but also agreed that Kelly had a iron clad case. With the witnesses they had on their side they had to be a conviction, even by this judge. They did wonder why Hudson kept asking if the witnesses had been to the holler and had asked Melinda about the grave.

When the trial resumed that afternoon, Mason, the newly freed slave of Custus McClung was called to the stand. He testified to seeing the smoke, hitching a wagon, loading it with buckets and several men and hurrying down the mountain road to the holler cabin that was burning out of control and was already beyond saving. He told of seeing the three defendants mounting their horses and leaving their dead brother on the ground, left the holler in a flat out run. He said Mr. McClung was dead in his buggy with three gunshot wounds in his chest. His empty double barreled shotgun was lying on the floor of the buggy and his horse was pacing up and down in its traces nervously. Sammie Winslow was dead on the ground in front of the burning house and Mrs. Lewis was sobbing and shaking in fright.

"What did you do Mason?" he was asked.

"Wasn't nothing to do, sir, Mr. McClung was already gone and the house was burning so fast we couldn't put the fire out. All we could do after a while was try to keep the fire off the out buildings so they wouldn't burn up too. After a while Mr. Blake he come and tell us what he wants done. Mrs. Lewis, she couldn't stop crying long enough to tell us what to do."

Kelly said he had no more questions and Hudson began questioning the witness for the defense.

"When you came down the mountain, Mason, did you hear shots from down below?"

"Yes sir, I did hear shots."

"And how many shots did you hear, Mason"? Hudson asked.

"I could not say for sure, sir. The noise coming from the wagon and horses drowned out a lot of the sound, I just knew they was shooting going on down there," said Mason.

"Did you see any one actually fire a shot, were there guns in any ones hands that you could see when you came up on the scene, Mason?"

"When I got in sight of the cabin they were already on their horses and I did not see guns in their hands at that time, sir."

"Were you close enough to see the faces of the men on the horses? Can you positively identify these men sitting here as the three men you saw ride out of the bottom that morning? Answer me, Mason and remember you can't think that's them, you have to be able to say absolutely to the exclusion of every other male on the earth that these are the men you saw that morning." Hudson leaned forward in anticipation of the answer.

Mason looked at Kelly for help and Kelly looked down at the floor. After a pause and a sigh, Mason had to say that they looked like the men but he was to far away to say that they were positively the men who rode away from the burning house. Then, Hudson asked him if he had seen the grave on the knoll and did he know whose grave it was.

"I have seen the grave on the knoll but I do not know who is in it, sir."

"No more questions, your honor."

Kelly called to the stand a very nervous and embarrassed Sidney Sammons. He placed his hand on the bible and swore to tell the truth and was seated in the witness stand. He was asked where he was from June 4th to June tenth of that year. He answered that he was here in Lewisburg. And what business were you here about that week, he was asked.

"I was not here on business," answered Sammons," I was here on pleasure at least it started out that way. I was here to get drunk."

The crowd laughed and Sammon's face reddened noticeably. Judge Holmes pounded the bench with the gavel and called for order.

"And you did get drunk Mr. Sammons?" Kelly asked gently, "and you did get put in the county jail? Is that correct, sir?"

"You know I did, Kelly."

"Tell us what happened, Sidney in your own words," Kelly instructed him.

"Well, I was drunk for about four days when one of the deputies stumbled on my feet that was sticking out of the hay down at the livery stable and I guess it made him mad cause he roused me from my nap and put me in the jail. Which was probably a good thing, at least I was in a bed. When I woke up the next morning one of them fellers there gave me his coffee after I drank mine. He found out where I was from and asked me a bunch of questions about what I would do to get rid of a body and strange stuff like that. Then he told me he had killed Mr. McClung and began laughing in the most disrespectful way. He said he and his brothers had shot him three times in the chest. I didn't even know Mr. McClung was dead and was shocked to death by him saying that and then laughing like a hyena about it. I screamed for the guard and they let me out and I was so glad to get away from them fellers. They murdered the best man I ever knew and then showed him disrespect on top of that. That's all I have to say about that sitiation." Sidney stated emphatically.

"Do you mean situation, Sidney?" asked Kelly.

"Yes sir, sitiation," answered Sidney. The defense then took over the questioning.

Hudson asked him, "Mr. Sammons you said that one of the men told you he killed Mr. McClung, is that correct? Which man, is he in the courtroom?"

"Yes sir, that one there, that mean one." He pointed at the older brother, Basil.

"That man said he killed McClung? Do you recall his exact words, Mr. Sammons? Think carefully now and if so repeat them for the court just like Winslow said them to you." Hudson seemed to be challenging Sidney's memory in front of the entire courtroom.

"I remember it like it was yesterday, He asked me if I knew Custus McClung from up that way and I said I sure did, just like I told everybody about Custus that he was the finest man I know. Then I asked him how he knew Custus and he said I know him cause I killed him just the other day. I put three shots in his chest while he sat in a buggy and then he started with that hyena laugh." Sidney said emphatically. "That's what he said, word for word."

"All right then," said Hudson. "So he said I killed him just the other day. Just like any man would say if he had shot some one in self defense. He did not say he murdered McClung, he said I killed McClung. By the way have you ever been in the place where the shootout took place? Have you seen the fresh grave on the knoll and do you know who is buried there?"

"You tricked me." Sidney said softly.

"Answer the questions, please Mr. Sammons, a bout the grave on the knoll."

"Yes, I've seen the grave. I do not know whose it is." Sidney said brokenly.

I'm through with this witness your honor," Hudson said as he walked back to his chair past a grinning Basil Winslow.

The judge adjourned the court for the day and the crowd filed out of the courthouse with conversation buzzing. This defense lawyer was so far doing a good job rebutting the prosecution testimony. Everybody in the crowd knew the Winslow's were guilty of murder and would be found so but the defense seemed to be heading for a self defense angle.

Over dinner that night at the Sweet Shop they all tried to cheer Nancy up and assure her she would do fine the next day. The district attorney had told her she would be on the stand first thing the next morning. He said that the defense lawyer would lean on her hard after Kelly finished with his questions.

It was very important to his case if he could rattle her while on the stand. She would undoubtedly be accused of all kinds of illicit behavior that he of course could not prove, but his purpose would be to try to make her look bad in front of the judge. He advised her to be calm and remember she was one of the victims here and not to forget that no matter how hard Hudson would try to show the court otherwise.

The next morning at 9:00 she was indeed called to the stand by Kelly. He started with the usual questions, her name, where she lived and so on. Then he asked if she had ever seen the defendants before and where and when.

"I saw these three men and their now dead brother for the first time when they came to my and my husbands home on Roaring Creek above Lewis Mill. I had been washing clothes when they appeared and began asking me questions about another brother of theirs that was missing and had been for some time. They wanted to know where my husband was and when he would be back. I told them I knew nothing about their brother and my husband was near by cutting wood in the forest and would be back shortly. I lied to them, hoping the threat of my husband returning would cause them to leave without hurting me. He was not cutting wood he had gone with his brother to Covington to return some mules he had borrowed."

"Who seemed to be in charge of the group? Who of the men did most of the talking?" Kelly asked.

"That one there," she said and pointed directly at Basil, "He did almost all of the talking. The more questions he asked me the angrier he seemed to get and after awhile he was like a maniac. One of the others came in while they were ransacking the house and said he had found a fresh grave on the knoll. That's when that man just about went crazy he started accusing me of carrying on with his brother and said that was his brother's grave they had found. He said my husband must have come home from the war and killed him and buried him there on the knoll. I tried to tell him we had just gotten married in May after the end of the war. I just came to the holler less than thirty days ago. He was having nothing of that and told the others to burn down the house. He laughed insanely and dragged me out the front door and into the front yard. He said the smoke would bring my husband and when it did he would kill him."

"And then what happened?" asked Kelly.

"When we were out side of the house and he was holding me and I was kicking and screaming, we looked up and Custus, Mr. McClung come riding up in his buggy. Two of them drew out their pistols and shot at Mr. McClung."

"Which of the two brothers shot at McClung initially? Could you tell who shot first?" Kelly asked her.

"Yes, sir, I know that the one called Basil fired because he was holding me with his left arm and shot with his right hand. That one fired also," she pointed at Lawrence. "They drew first and shot and missed Custus with their first shots. Then the brother who was killed drew his gun and shot but he also missed, I believe. Custus pulled out his shotgun and killed the one who shot last. He was the closest to him. That one there, that is crippled, then drew his gun and Custus shot him in the foot. Then they all three that was still living, shot Custus right in the chest, it was three shots, that looked like a pyramid." She touched her self three times in the shape of a pyramid.. Her voice was starting to break and tears were welling up in her eyes.

"You are certain the Winslow's shot first, Mrs. Lewis."

"Absolutely certain," said Nancy. "Custus yelled out, what's going on here", when he reined in his horse and they started shooting. He was trying to help me and they just murdered him. Then they saw the Negro men from Twin Sugars Plantation coming down the road and they jumped on their horses and took off. They burned our home to the ground. I guess that's something they got used to doing during the war and can't get enough of it."

"Objection, your honor, said Hudson.

"Sustained, "said Holmes. "Please keep your personal opinions of the defendants to your self, Mrs. Lewis."

"I have no further questions for this witness at this time, Your Honor, but I reserve the right to recall her at a later time," stated Kelly.

"Duly noted,"grunted Holmes. Then he called for lunch recess and said for everyone to return in one hour ready for the cross examination by the defense.

Hudson began his cross examination of Nancy by asking her why she told the Winslow's that her husband was close by that day. Did she not know they would only wait until he came back if they thought he knew something about their missing brother?

Nancy said that she thought just the opposite was true, that they might leave if they thought her husband was close by to protect her. She said that her first instinct would always be to tell a stranger that someone was nearby so it would appear that she was not really alone. He then asked her if she herself felt some responsibility for what happened that day. No, she did not feel responsible, Nancy retorted. Those men came to her house and started the whole incident and she would never take any responsibility for what those animals sitting across the room from her had done.

"But if the grave had not been there, do you think the situation would have escalated to the point that death would be a result?" Hudson asked.

"I don't understand", Nancy replied. "How could I be responsible for the grave being there?

"Someone is responsible for the grave, Mrs. Lewis. Who is buried there?"

"I do not know who is buried in that grave, and my husband does not know who is buried there." Nancy testified.

"Could it be Mrs. Lewis that the grave contains the body of Bill Winslow, the brother of these three men on trial here today and Basil Winslow was right when he suspected you of hiding something? Could that be correct Mrs. Lewis?"

"Like I just said I do not know who is in that grave. If it is true Bill Winslow is buried there I still know nothing of what happened to him". Nancy said.

Hudson said, "Now Mrs. Lewis you stated that when Mr. McClung rode up in the yard of your house in his buggy that Basil Winslow had his, I believe you said, left arm around you and he drew his pistol with his right hand. Is that correct Mrs. Lewis?"

She nodded yes, and said that was correct.

"So, he was holding you so you could not run back into the burning house. Is that correct, Mam? He was keeping you from harming yourself and your neighbor seeing you held by a strange man and you fighting against him so forcefully got the wrong impression and thought Mr. Winslow was trying to harm you. He drew his shotgun and shot to protect his poor distraught neighbor. Didn't he Mrs. Lewis?" asked Hudson in a rush of words so Nancy could not interrupt him until he could say his piece.

"No, no, he was restraining me but it was so I could not run away. He wanted me there with him so Clarke would come and he could kill him," said Nancy.

"Isn't it true that the fire started when you became so upset with Basil Winslow that you threw an oil lamp at him and it shattered and spread fire all over the first floor. I submit Mrs. Lewis that you started the fire accidentally and Mr. Winslow had to carry you outside the house to the yard and restrain you in order to keep you from rushing back in to the house. You were so distraught over losing the wedding items, that you had just received on your wedding day as gifts from friends and relatives that you were disregarding your own safety that day. Answer me truthfully Mrs. Lewis," demanded Hudson in a raised voice.

"That's not true," said Nancy. "He was like a maniac and was waiting for my husband Clarke Lewis so he could shoot him down. How many times must I say it?"

Disregarding her answer, Hudson said, "So when McClung saw this scene he began shooting and killed one brother with one barrel of the shotgun and crippled this poor young man, probably for life before they could draw their guns and defend themselves. Their return fire was accurate and they killed poor

Mr. McClung in a tragic, tragic incident that was no more than an accident. So, so sad," he shook his head and looked down at the floor in such a mournful way. "I have no more questions, Your Honor."

Kelly said he had a question for Mrs. Lewis. "Are you absolutely sure that these events happened just the way you testified? That the Winslow's started the fire in your house and that they fired first at Custus McClung?"

Nancy looked back at him and never blinked. "The Winslow's started the fire in order to draw my husband home and they shot at Mr. McClung before he even picked up his shotgun. So help me, God." She was excused from the stand on that note.

Judge Holmes said the trial was over for the day and the defense would be calling their first witness the next morning.

Nancy was so relieved for her part of the trial to be over she could hardly eat that evening. The prosecutor joined the four for dinner along with the Morgan's and he stated that Nancy had done a magnificent job on the stand that day. The way he saw it the Winslow's were conceding they were there that day and did the shooting. The whole trial came down to whether the judge believed Nancy or the Winslow's as to who shot first and to who started the fire on the arson charge. For the first time he hinted that the possibility of a fair shake from the judge might be an issue. He told them the judge was sent in from Wheeling just to try this case. They all were adamant that justice for Custus had to be forth coming from this trial. Kelly said they had presented more than enough evidence to convict the brothers and if the judge did not find them guilty then everyone would know for certain that the whole trial was just a carpetbagger scam going all the way to new governor's office. He said he did not think the new judge would stay in town after this trial no matter how the verdict went. The people of Greenbrier County had elected Judge Hailey and as long as he was healthy he would in most instances be trying cases again. Some one brought up the question of whether he thought the judges were switched because Custus was such a popular and beloved citizen or because of the Winslow brothers connections. He said that it was probably some of both. The powerful men in Wheeling knew how popular Custus was with the population and would be almost sure to convict the Winslow's of his murder. But, no matter what low life bandits the Winslow brothers were they had some strong influence in the new government and if they should happen to get off, God forbid, who knew what they might do next.

They would truly know then they could do any thing their twisted minds could conceive and the law would protect them to the end.

Morning three of the trial opened with lawyer Hudson calling Basil Winslow to the stand. In direct contradiction to the behavior he had exhibited in Lewis Mill on his tirade to find his brother. Basil was very calm and almost cordial in his demeanor. He identified himself and answered all the usual questions, what he did for a living etc. Hudson then brought him along up to the time of the brother's arrival in the holler. He conveniently left out the part of him beating Blake and cursing Melinda and the three men at the store. He asked Basil to relate in his own words what had happened when they arrived at the Lewis cabin beside the creek.

"Well sir, me and my three brothers were trying to find my brother Bill who was one year younger than I am, me being the oldest of the family. He had been missing going on three weeks and we put together what he had told each of us. Just little bits and pieces told to each one over the last few months. He was seeing a woman whose husband was in the Reb army. She lived up a creek somewhere in the Cold Knob area and that's pretty much all we knew. We were terribly worried about Bill because he had never been gone away for that long before."

"How did you happen to go to the Lewis house, Basil?" asked his lawyer.

"No reason, we were just riding up side roads that had some kind of a creek near it and we came up on this house. We asked the lady of the house if she knew any thing about Brother Bill and she got nervous real fast like. She told us her husband was out cutting wood and would be back very soon and he would take care of us when he got back. She said it like we were trying to hurt her or something. One of my brother's I think it was Sammie, said he found a fresh grave above the house on a knoll." Basil was just as low key and earnest as he could be as he told his story.

"Where were you when this conversation was taking place?" asked Hudson.

"We were in the house, I had just stepped in side the living room door. When the finding of the grave was brought up the lady just seemed to lose control and started pacing back and forth. It was obvious that she was very nervous about us finding the grave. She began screaming at me to get out of her house and that her husband would kill us all when he got there. Then she grabbed a lamp that was there on a small table and threw it at me, I was able to dodge it but it was lit and the kerosene went everywhere when it hit the wall. The flames flared up the sides of the walls and the house began burning like a kindling fire."

"What happened next? You all ran out of the house I am sure," said Hudson.

"No sir. The fire seemed to bring her back to earth. She began to gather up things to take out side. Help me," she said. "I've got to get all my wedding presents out before the fire gets to them. The flames were going crazy and she would not leave the house. I finally had to pick her up bodily and carry her screaming from the house to the front yard. She wouldn't give up trying to get back in the burning house, poor thing. She was so upset over those wedding gifts." Basil seemed so sympathetic to the poor girl's misery.

Nancy, Clarke and nearly everyone in the court room was seething at this murderer's lies and acting. He was a masterful liar and if they had not known better he would have had them believing his fabricated story. Nancy had to bite her lip to keep from exploding and saying out loud what a liar and lout he was.

"You were holding her back and she wanted to run back into the inferno that had been her house. Is that what you're saying Mr. Winslow?" asked Hudson.

"That's exactly what I am saying," Basil continued, "I saved that poor woman's life and she was in such a state of shock she probably does not even remember my generosity." He turned and looked at Nancy with deep concern and pity on his face.

"You're lying, you're lying," Nancy screamed out. Holmes pounded the bench with his gavel and yelled, "Order in the court, order in the court."

"Your honor, we ask for the poor woman's outburst to be stricken from the courts record, She obviously had no control of herself at that moment. She is not her self." Hudson magnanimously offered up to the court.

"Proceed with questioning," barked Holmes. "We will tolerate no more outbursts in this courtroom."

"So when Mr. McClung came up on the scene, he saw you restraining Mrs. Lewis and came in shooting. Is that what you are prepared to say, Mr. Winslow?" asked Hudson.

"Yes, because that's what happened. I guess he thought I was holding her captive with the house burning and all and he did what any good friend and neighbor would have done. He shot two of my poor brothers killing poor little Sammie and crippling little Ross. I should never have brought them to that place. I feel that it was all my fault and I will regret this incident to my last days," He began sobbing brokenly, saying through his tears, "all my fault, all my fault.

What an actor that son-of-a-bitch is, went through many of the spectators minds and they looked at him with silence and anger, not the sympathy his acting was designed to bring forth.

"Take your time and compose your self Mr. Winslow," his attorney said and an awkward three minutes passed as the witness stopped his sobbing and trumpeted a snot filled blow in to the silk handkerchief handed him by Hudson. "When you are ready you can continue with the details of the shootings. Who shot first and who shot McClung?"

Winslow took so long to continue that some in the audience thought that maybe he was distraught over the death of his brother. Perhaps he had the mental strength to save his mourning until now and was using the forum of the witness stand to accomplish two things, mourn for his little brother and gain sympathy at the same time in this crucial part of the trial. He finally continued with:

"After McClung shot my first brother we all drew our guns and started shooting at him in self defense. He then shot Ross and we were able to shoot him in the chest three times before he could pull his pistol out of his hidden holster and injure us more. We shot in self defense and he died because of a tragic error on his part. All we were trying to do was find our lost brother and trouble was the last thing we wanted. We are sorry that a good man died, but two good men died that day and all we did was ask a question of a backward mountain woman who probably belonged in a insane asylum."

The crowd erupted in a cacophony of shouts and slurs. They were taking no more insults from this band of Yankee trash and they only got louder as the judge pounded his gavel and called for order again. They only quieted down when Sheriff Knight and his deputies entered the courtroom with cocked shot guns. Judge Holmes then called for a recess of sixty minutes to cool things off. He ordered that the courtroom be emptied of all spectators. Tempers and emotions were sky high as the crowd went out side and milled around under the giant shade trees that lined the streets around the courthouse. No one really felt like eating but a few went through the motions. More than one opinion was expressed that the shit eating judge from Wheeling was going to let the murderers of Custus McClung walk away scot free.

Some felt they had fought one war against the Yankee's and lost and now they were losing the war for justice for their friend.

The trial convened one hour from the time of the dismissal and Hudson stated he was finished with the witness. Kelly stepped forward for his turn with the defendant.

He asked Winslow, "If Mr McClung did, as you say, ride up and shoot your first brother dead and wound the next with two shots from his double barreled shot gun before you and your two other brothers even drew your guns. Why did you not let him live? He would have been sitting in his carriage with an empty shot gun. Did you feel it was necessary for you and your brothers to shoot him three times in the chest at point blank range.

"He was reaching for his pistol, we could take no chance that he would not shoot us too," said Basil.

"So you admit that the only gun McClung had in his hands was empty when you shot him three times in the chest." Kelly said with emphasis on empty.

"He had not pulled his pistol yet, but he meant to pull it." said Basil loudly with no trace of his earlier remorse.

"I have no more questions for this witness, Your Honor," said Kelly and walked away.

Hudson said he had no more witnesses to call and he wished to rest the defense. He was taking no chances with bringing Lawrence and Ross to the stand. He knew how difficult it was to get three defendants to answer every question the same way and he did not want to give Kelly the opportunity to poke holes in the other two stories. Basil had been able to convey remorse and almost got some sympathy but the two younger brothers were no where near as savvy as the wily experienced Basil.

CHAPTER 14

The Summation and Verdict

Kelly began his summation by saying the state had proved the Winslow's had killed Mr. McClung in cold blood. He went over all the witness testimony and placed them at the shooting site and had witnessed them leaving the site in a hurry.

They had proven the Winslow's had burned the Lewis home and restrained Nancy Lewis whom they thought would draw her husband in so they could extract revenge for what they thought was the murder of their brother. They had proven the defendants had shot and killed Custus McClung who came to the aid of his neighbor's wife. All this because they thought the grave on the Lewis property held the body of their brother. They had no proof that this was so. They had no proof that their brother was even dead and not simply gone off some place to get away from them. They even admitted on cross examination that the man they murdered in the buggy was holding only an empty shotgun. That is if you believe the story that Custus McClung rode up and just shot two of them for no reason except Basil was holding Nancy Lewis so she would not run back to the fire to retrieve a few material things. Mrs.

Lewis testified that she saw three Winslow's fire at Custus McClung for no reason when he came into the yard to help her. Some one fired first and some one returned fire to protect themselves. Let's look at the two sides and make a reasonable decision. Mr. McClung had lived on this earth for sixty nine years that day last month. No one ever knew him to kill any one for any reason in those sixty nine years. No one knew him to even threaten to kill any one in those sixty nine years. I ask you what would make him kill and wound one of the Winslow brothers that day. Because they were holding Nancy and the house was burning. He would have attempted to find out what was happening there. What did Mrs. Lewis say Custus said when he came up on the scene? She said that he wanted to know what was going on here? That is the response for any normal person, find out what was really happening, not, just start shooting people with a shot gun. I say that Mr. McClung would never have handled the situation that way. He would have shot only after one or all of them shot at him. Now, let's look at the other side in this situation. Nancy Lewis says Basil became agitated when the fresh grave was discovered and went crazy. She says, and I and 99% of the people in this room believe her, that they burned her house to attract her husband because she lied to them and told them her husband was close by and would come to protect her. They found the grave and they thought they had found their brothers body and solved the mystery. So I say they burned the house down, they killed Mr. McClung in cold blood and they held Nancy Lewis against her will. I ask the court to convict the defendants and ask for justice for the family and friends of Mr. Custus McClung late of Twin Sugars Plantation. Kelly concluded his closing statement on that note and turned the floor over to the defense attorney Mr. Hudson.

Hudson began, that the state would like you to believe that these men killed Custus McClung and I agree that they did kill him. They, themselves agree that they killed him. The defendants admit they were at the scene of the shooting, they admit that the house was burned down, that they killed

Mr. McClung, they admit that they restrained Mrs. Lewis. We have heard the testimony of Basil Winslow, of his regret, of his guilt for placing his younger brothers in harms way that day. We heard of his gallant act of keeping the obviously distraught Nancy Lewis from rushing in the inferno to save a few gifts. Basil is a hero, he saved this young woman's life that day and yet he is subjected to a trial that threatens his very life. We heard of his obvious grief and regret for having to help take the life of Mr. McClung who he says he never knew but feels acquainted with because of the deceased man's sterling reputation. As sterling as he was, when he fired with out provocation at the defendants that morning they had no choice but to defend themselves. The Winslow's are victims of a bizarre set of circumstances that robbed them of their brother's life and set them on a course that required their taking of the life of one of Greenbrier Counties most up right citizens statesmen of all times. Let's not go down that wrong road that leads to punishing these men for an event they could no more control than I can control the weather. Do the right thing and find these good men innocent by self defense and give some meaning to this terrible accident that was thrust on them that June morning. I leave this case in your capable hands, Your Honor."

Judge Holmes said that concluded the evidence portion of the case and he would make his decision by morning. He stated in open court that no matter what the verdict of the case turned out to be, he had issued a written order to the sheriff to have the mysterious grave in the Roaring Creek holler opened to determine who was buried there. He said this had no bearing on the verdict in the case in any way but since it had come up time and time again he had decided to put speculation to rest once and for all,

He said the court would convene at 11:00 the next day for the announcement of the verdict instead of the usual 9:00 a.m. Then he said a strange thing, he stated that the recent war had torn the country apart and caused many casualties on both sides. Now the war was over and the Southern way of life was over, not just because of the freedom of the slaves and the influx of Northern businessmen but the method of having one group of citizens think they could act independent of the central government. Every trial or event in this neighborhood of the state would be subject to scrutiny by and for the new state government and ultimately by the Federal government. This would be the way things were done here until the state was satisfied that the old Rebel ways were truly over and forgotten by even the most die-hard Confederate sympathizers. He said the citizens of Greenbrier could make it hard or easy on themselves, which ever way they decided to go in these next few years during the time that had been named Reconstruction. He said that martial law could be introduced and they could send in troops to maintain order but the government would prefer not to have to do that. The outburst that he witnessed in the courtroom was just such an incident that could require martial law and the introduction of troops to be stationed here full time. If that happened then trials like this would not be necessary, they would suspend habeus corpus and just lock up who they wanted, indefinitely and never have to bring them to trial. He said that he hoped for their sake this drastic step would not be necessary and they would become loyal and law abiding citizens. Then he adjourned the court for the day.

The trial had been an exhausting ordeal that every one wanted to put behind them and get on with their lives. Weeds were growing in the fields and needed chopping and orders for meal were backing up at the mill. John Morgan, Mabel's husband had cases to take care of, although his assistants were keeping his law firm going while he tended to his wife's families affairs. That evening the Morgan's and the Lewis brothers and their ladies had dinner at the General Lewis Inn. As they ate they tried to keep the conversation away from the trial and tried not to think about what the verdict might be on the following morning. Morgan however, brought up the lecture they had received from the judge that afternoon. He stated that what he was saying to them was what ever the verdict turned out to be they should accept it. The threat of stationing troops in Greenbrier and all the other things that came with it was real. They knew with out saying it that a lynch mob, should the case go against them, would be just the thing to cause the troops to be sent here. They all slept fitfully that night, anxious about the verdict and nervous about the crowds reaction to it.

Just before eleven o'clock the court room was unlocked and a few spectators entered early to get good seats. As eleven o'clock arrived there was no sign of the defendants or their lawyer. The only vacant seats in the court room were at the empty defendants table. People began talking between them of what it could mean. The court was called to order and every one was asked to rise for His Honor Judge Hailey, Hailey? What happened to Holmes? This must mean good things if their own Judge Hailey was back on the case. Judge Hailey began addressing the courtroom.

"This court is back in session for the final time in the case of The State of West Virginia vs Basil, Lawrence and Ross Winslow. Judge Holmes had made his decision and"

"Where's the defendants, Judge? Why ain't they here to hear the verdict? Someone in the crowd yelled out.

"I will get to that in a moment, and don't interrupt me again or I will clear the courtroom forceably, if need be. Now as I was saying a verdict in the case has been reached by the bench. On the charge of murder of arson, the court found the defendants not guilty." A roar went up in the courtroom and the judge banged the gavel for silence. "On the charge of forceable restraint the court finds a verdict of not guilty." The crowd moaned but waited for the big verdict. "On the charge of murder the court finds not guilt by reason of self defense." This time the crowd again roared but louder than before. Some of them screamed at the top of their voices and shook their fists at the judge. It took five minutes for the noise to dissipate enough for the judge to continue. Constant banging of the gavel was followed with the deputies and their shot guns entering the court room again and eventually the judge was able to quiet them down enough to resume speaking.

"This was the verdict passed on this case by the sitting judge. Judge Holmes had already left the county. The prisoners have been released from custody."

More curses came from the crowd and Judge Hailey had to pound the gavel again. The deputies stepped toward the crowd and after a few moments, order was again restored.

"This trial is over fellow citizens. There is, if you will allow me a few moments, some things I would like to express. As you well know, I have been a loyal Virginian and supported the Confederacy in the recent war as most of you have. We laid down our arms and surrendered to the Federal government and in so doing we also surrendered to the new State of West Virginia goverment. The eyes of that goverment are now looking at our county. Judge Holmes informed me of the warning he gave of the possibility of armed troops being sent to this region. I know many of you do not approve of the verdicts in this trial. I am here this morning to ask, as one of you, that you not try to enact revenge outside the law in this court case. Every one here is suffering the pain of seeing defendants that you feel were proved guilty, not be punished. Some times the law works that way, we do not have to like it. But, despite the perceived injustice that you feel happened here, please do not do any thing that would precipitate the sending of Federal troops here. The pain of injustice you feel now would pale in comparison to the injustice you would see if the writ of habeas corpus is enacted. Judge Holmes or some one like him would be sent here to exact their revenge. Many, many of you good people would be sent to prison with out a trial or even charges ever being brought against you. That, my fellow citizens, would be much harsher, for the whole county, than what you are now suffering. Please go to your homes and try to let this tragic epic in the history of our county die the death of all such injustice. This court is dismissed." Judge Hailey said and rapped the gavel one last time.

John Morgan and Mabel rose from their seats and begged for the crowd's attention. Mabel began speaking:

"Dear friends," she said. "My husband and I spoke until late last night of the possibility that this court may let my father's murderers go free. As painful as that reality is this morning, we came to the conclusion that if this moment did indeed come we would ask you to accept it as the cruel fate it is. We know that the Winslow's are cruel murderers, but we also know that what Judge Hailey and Holmes said was true. Retribution by any of us would bring such a firestorm and punishment this county may never survive it. We have suffered for four years at the hand of this vicious bunch of Yankee scum and now we must endure more. My father would not want the whole area to suffer to avenge his loss. My family asks and the Lewis family asks that you not retaliate in any way against the Winslow's. They will suffer for their sins in the next life if not in this one. Justice will find a way to be carried out in some fashion some day, but let's not let it be from us. Please do not bring the State and Federal government's wrath up on our innocent citizens, I implore you. Thank you from the bottom of my heart for the outpouring of support you have shown my dad and my family."

The courtroom was silent for a moment and then someone stood and clapped their hands. Then everyone stood and applauded the daughter of Custus McClung who stood with her husband and Nancy and Clarke Lewis with tears of gratitude in their eyes. They would show their respect for Mr. McClung by letting the past remain the past. Fresh though the pain of loss was, they knew the healing process was beginning at the moment she finished speaking.

They all decided they would not pass the Double Cross in Frankford and chance having to see the three Winslow brothers walking free. They went out the James River and Kanawha Turnpike and then turned right on the Rader's Valley Road. They followed it to the Floyd Bobbitt residence and again turned right and passed over Culbertson Creek and rejoined the Williamsburg Frankford road. They passed the horse shoe curve and looked down on the country residence of Sheriff Knight. They had forgotten about the order Judge Malcolm had given Knight to exhume the body in the grave in the holler. Seeing his house sparked a conversation about that unpleasant duty that would soon be performed by a group of diggers and probably numerous onlookers. Nancy remarked that this whole episode seemed like a night mare that went on and on with out end. The shock of what happened at the shooting site, the burial of Custus, the loss of their home and now the realization that Basil Winslow and his brother's would never be punished sometimes seemed to much to bear. She asked Clarke what would happen if Bill Winslow was buried on the knoll. Would this whole night mare begin again? Would they now charge them with murder if he had been killed somehow? He tried to reassure her but she lapsed into a long silence and let the series of doubts and questions she had dance around in her head.

Chapter 15

The Exhumation

Everyone felt glad to be back in Lewis Mill. They drifted apart and each one returned to their homes to resume their lives. Nancy and Clarke returned to Carr's farmhouse and everyone, despite the outcome, was glad the ordeal of the trial was finally over. The resumption of their lives with out Winslow influence lasted three days. They were just finishing breakfast when the sheriff's deputy rode up and told them they were down in the holler exhuming the grave. They decided to walk through the woods and let the deputy return down the road by himself. They could go over the hill by the vacant home of his distant relative called the Dick Place. Just below it they rejoined the road and arrived at the burned out shell of their former home in just over six minutes.

They were greeted by the sheriff and three deputies along with four laborers they had picked up along the way. Two wagons were nearby in anticipation of transporting the remains. Two men were already down in the hole to just above their waists throwing shovelfuls of the rich black dirt up out of the hole. It was easy digging since the earth had not had time to even pack down tight again from the first time it had been removed. While they watched the workers excavate the grave they talked with Sheriff Knight who told them how much he hated to see the Winslow brothers escape justice. They just nodded, they really did not want to talk about the trial again. The two of them had made a kind of pact, whereby they would not talk about the trial or any part of what had taken place for awhile.

Horses were heard approaching and they both gasped when they looked up and right there before them sat Basil and Lawrence Winslow and two other men on their horses. Basil was smiling down at them in that sick sneer he had hidden during the trial.

"Why good morning, folks," he said. " I see the sheriff is finally doing his assigned duty."

"Get out of here Winslow, Get off my land and I do mean now. "Clarke said in a low growl. "Get them out of here right now, Sheriff."

"We have a right to be here, Sheriff. That's our brother you're digging up and I want to make sure you don't lose the body, if you know what I mean, Sheriff? Here, how about this," he threw the top three rails of the line fence down on the ground and stepped his horse across the fence. "Now, we ain't on your land and we can still keep an eye on things. Won't be no trouble that way. Come on across, boys," he said to the other three and they also jumped the two rails remaining of the fence.

The Lewis's both were shaking with anger. Clarke looked at Basil with hatred in his eyes, as he did he could see himself plunging a knife into his chest, the way he had been forced to do on occasion during the war. He knew he could kill this man in an instance and feel no remorse. What he had taken from him, seeing his wife humiliated here in the holler, on the witness stand and the burning of his lifetime home had awakened something in side him that he thought had died at Winchester. He had intended to never kill again but this animal smiling at him from just across the fence had awakened the animalistic feeling he though he had buried forever.

"Hell Sheriff," one of the laborers hollered up from down in the grave. "There ain"t no body down here. I'm down almost six feet already and there's nothing here unless they buried a sparrow down here."

The sheriff walked to the edge of the grave and looked down. "Have you reached the end of the loose dirt yet? I mean the dirt that was thrown back in to the grave at first."

"I'm back on hardpan dirt right here." and he plunged the shovel into the dirt about three inches. He began scraping the loose dirt up from the compacted earth. "This right here is as far down as they dug. This grave's empty Sheriff." He threw his shovel up to the surface and reached up with his right hand and was hoisted up out of the grave. "There was a coffin down there though, I could see wood chips offen the box. Some body's done moved this one on you, sir."

"I knew it, I knew it," screamed Basil. "You dillydallied around and gave these people time to move my brother's body. That judge was stupid to say anything about the grave in open court. Now they done dug him up. Where is he? Where is he? He screamed at Nancy and Clarke.

"Sheriff, we don't know anything about this grave." Clarke said, "I will swear it on a bible."

"I want them both arrested right now," yelled Basil. "I knew they were up to something." He looked at Clarke and said, "You know if you had been cutting wood that day, you would have been dead right along with that meddling neighbor of yours."

Cold stare and no answer was the response he got from Clarke.

The sheriff told Basil to move along and he would certainly not be arresting any one now. There was no evidence they had done anything and furthermore what would be the charge. He said for the Winslow's to move on down the road and let him worry about arrests and charges. That was not their business, missing brother or not. When they did not move out he then told them he was losing patience with them and judge in their back pocket or not, if they did not leave the premises immediately he would show them a fight a damn sight bloodier that the one they started here the last time.

They jumped the fence in to the road and started down toward the bend of the road when Basil reined in and turned back to Sheriff Knight.

"We are leaving here this time sheriff, but you listen to me. Some one in this valley knows what happened to our brother Bill and I aim to find out who that someone is. You hear me, lawman?" he asked and did not wait for an answer before he spurred his horse forward and was soon out of sight around the bend in the road.

Clarke told the sheriff he wasn't sure how much more he was going to take from that murdering bunch. The sheriff asked him to hold off retaliating against Basil, he hoped some thing might turn up that would help them solve the disappearance of Bill Winslow. They again talked of what could have happened to the body in the grave. The sheriff said this was turning out to be the most baffling incident he had witnessed while in office. The laborers were back to work refilling the hole with dirt and when they were finished the grave looked just like before, forlorn, deserted and lonely.

When Basil, Lawrence and the two hired toughs with them rode down to Lewis Mill they had decided to investigate the sinkhole that Sidney Sammons had told them about. They were looking for some one who could direct them to it and just below the store they rode up on Carl Blake the man that Basil had rope whipped about the face on their last trip up Roaring Creek, the day of the Custus McClung shooting. If he had seen them in advance Carl might have run from the encounter, but he did not and they, nor him, would ever know for sure if he would have darted away. Basil delighted in seeing the man he so obviously loathed before him as before, walking while he was mounted above him.

"Well, if it's not the rope beaten Mr. Blake. Tell me Mr. Blake what caused that awful man to beat you so, for no reason" He mimicked Kelly the prosecutor.

"I don't know Mr. Prosecutor I was so kind and nice to him." He mocked in a high voice. " Tell me Blake, where is the Sivvey Hole? If you give me instructions I might not whip your sorry ass again," Basil said.

"What they call the Sivvey Hole is the sinks of the crick. You take a right out this road go just a little ways and cross the bridge. After you cross the bridge, take a left and follow the crick about 600 yards. You will come right to it." Blake spoke quickly showing little emotion.

"I sure do appreciate that information, Mr. Blake." Basil tipped his hat towards Carl and then swung his right foot out and kicked Carl on the side of the jaw. "I'll show you what a snake that testifies against me gets." He began beating Carl who had fallen on the ground with the same rope he had used before on him. He flogged him about the head and face and blood began flowing in to the dusty road. Carl rolled over and tried to cover his face and head the best he could with his hands but the constant flailing never abated.

"Hold it, stop beating that man," said Carr Lewis as he stood there in his white miller's apron with flour covering his face and arms with a shot gun pointed at Basil. "Stop hitting him and back away now."

Basil stopped with his right arm raised above his head to strike another blow. He looked at the open double barrels of the shot gun pointed at his head and forced himself to lower the looped rope. He slowly wrapped the rope around his arm tightening the loops back in a neat tight bundle and hooked it on his saddle horn.

"I know you Reb, I saw you at that spring below Frankford. You're a brother to the asshole whose house I burned down. This ain't your business," Winslow said quietly. Then he grinned that sort of sick sneer that turned one side of his mouth down and the other up. "Besides, we were just asking for some directions and things got a little out of hand."

"Move on," Carr stated flatly.

Carl Blake staggered to his feet and told Basil, "You've beat me like a dog two times now." His left eye was swelling shut and blood still ran down his chin from a nasty cut on his busted lip. The welts on his forehead and cheeks were white against the deep red of the rest of his face. "If you try to beat me a third time, I promise you that you will die. You will not beat me again Winslow," Blake said this in the same calm voice he would have used to recite The Lord's Prayer on Sunday morning.

Basil Winslow tilted his head back and laughed the long cackle he always used followed by a series of he, he he's. He backed his horse up two steps and kicked him in the sides and moved on down the road , laughing and looking back at the shotgun the whole time. They used the beaten Blake's directions and crossed the bridge and went south down a large flat hay field that had just been cut for the summers first harvest.

Carr helped Carl Blake in to the kitchen of his small house and cleaned him as best as he could. He found two small beef steaks to place on his eye and lip to keep the swelling down. He hated to see such a nice man be subjected to such a beating by a maniac like Winslow. Melinda brought some laudanum for the pain and Blake fell asleep on the davenport sofa in the front room. How could the law allow some one like the Winslow's to run free and abuse good law abiding citizens like Carl Blake. Carl slept three hours and awoke to smell potato soup on the stove being stirred by Melinda. As he tried to eat some they brought up the possibility of getting the law involved. He said there was no way he would go back to Lewisburg and testify against Basil in another trial and watch him walk free again. No, he said calmly, next time I encounter him I will be carrying my pistol and if he tries to make it three times on my head, he will not bother any of us again. He said that with such finality that conversation stopped for a period of time. Melinda said after a long silence that perhaps it would not come to that, maybe Winslow would just leave the valley after he realized his missing brother was gone. As they ate their potato soup quietly, each one mulled that possibility in their minds and just as quietly dismissed it as being wishful thinking.

CHAPTER 16

The Sievey Hole

The sinks of the creek known locally as the Seivey Hole, was a huge dumping ground for what ever was caught up and swept along in the raging brown waters when the creek was high from rain in the mountains. All the little streams and creeks that fed the larger stream would cause the waters to come boiling down the valley sweeping up anything that the undulating waters could move. The water would pool around the hole in the earth's surface and create an instant lake with a whirlpool in the bottom that sucked everything down under the surface. Very much like a sieve which allowed some things to pass through and others to gather around the opening. When the incoming water from Roaring Creek would slow enough to allow the extra accumulated water in the instant lake to recede down the hole, an ever changing landscape would result. Every where the instant lake had been there would be a vast sea of dried mud after a few days. Huge rocks plus tree limbs and boards, farm wagons and parts of chicken coops and all sorts of human debris would be scattered around the docile, now almost peaceful hole. Each time the creek would swell from heavy rains the scene would play out over and over again. Over time the opening grew deeper and the rocks, trees and debris grew higher and higher until descending to the hole was like climbing down a huge tree.

When the Winslow's reached the sinks they dismounted and walked in to the chasm. "What a huge asshole of a place this is," announced Lawrence, with his voice bouncing off the sides of the gorge in an echo. "Hello, hello," he yelled out, "Is anyone here but bats and hoot owls?" Owls, owls, owls, went the echo. Scattered around were a few articles of clothing that the water and current had reduced to rags. Basil walked ahead like he was going to a fire, ten steps ahead of the others. He looked down in to the opening as if he expected to see a body at any time. About twenty feet down in the mass of tree limbs that resembled a giant brush pile, he spied something that looked familiar hanging on a tree limb.

"Look," he said to Lawrence. "That's Bill's vest hanging down on that tree limb. I'll be go to hell if it,ain't." Lawrence agreed that it did indeed look like the favorite article in Bill's wardrobe. He wore that vest on all but the very hottest day's of the year. It was an unusual article of clothing, with different shades of leather ranging from the dark chocolate to the light tan. It was all sewed together in alternating shades, even the texture of each piece was different, smooth to rough. All textures were represented in the vest.

"Go down there and get that vest, Roland," he ordered the young man who accompanied them. Roland looked at the pile of limbs and tree trunks in a jumbled mass and began looking for the best way to get to the vest. He descended carefully, picking his way along, he stepped gingerly on each branch and limb, testing it for firmness before applying his full weight.

"Cock and ass, boy. Are you going to take all day?" Basil yelled down when his impatience got the better of him. Roland did not answer, he just ignored the older man and continued to pick his way down through the tangle of rotten wood that had been there for decades. As mean as he knew Basil was, his threats could not compare to what awaited him if one of the dried out limbs would break with a pop and drop him in to the hole and down to who knows what was waiting below that surface. He reached the vest hanging on a dry locust branch and carried it with him as he just as gingerly ascended up through the limbs. When he reached the top Basil was impatiently reaching for it and snatched it from his outreached hand. Holding the vest in his hands he turned it over and over as if he couldn't believe it was Bills. He reached in to the pockets on each side near the waist and also felt in the inside breast pocket. He fished out something and said in a surprisingly subdued tone, "It's Bills all right, this is his metal toothpick he always carried."

He held the toothpick up for all to see. It was made of metal, probably steel, and must have belonged to Bill Winslow. It was carried in a small wooden vial with rounded edges on each end. The carrying of a metal toothpick was something very few men did and was a peculiar habit. All of them had seen him fish it out of the vest pocket after a meal. Stamped in the leather on the inside of the vest in black letters was McCoy's Leather, Williamsburg, West Virginia. Basil knew that was where Bill had his vest made. That advertisement and the steel toothpick would serve to convince even the most pessimistic observer. It had to belong to Bill Winslow with out a doubt.

"It looks like this is where poor old Bill ended up," said Basil. "Let's spread out and see if we can find anything else".

They spent the better part of two hours searching in the mud and muck left over from the floodwaters. Nothing else of interest was found, no more clothing that looked familiar and most important no human remains. One of them even walked in the knee deep mud to peer down in to the dark opening of the Seivey Hole looking for some sign of Bill, but nothing was found. They then rode out hard toward Frankford and reached the Double Cross at dusk. They drank heavily that night and reminisced about their two dead brothers and drunkenly toasted their memory. In their minds Sammie had been ruthlessly shot down by Custus McClung. They downplayed the fact that they all shot first to the point it never happened that way at all. Basil said they would ride to Lewisburg the next morning and see the worthless sheriff and show him Bills vest. They would also send a telegram to Judge Holmes telling him of the empty grave and finding Bills vest at the sinkhole.

Chapter 17

You Won't Beat Me Again

Clarke and Nancy walked back up the road from the grave opening incident. They were both deeply affected by seeing the Winslow brothers back on their land again. They could not, no matter how much they thought and talked of it, come up with an answer to the grave mystery. How someone could have been buried there and they not know whom was a mystery in its self. They had noticed the fresh grave two days after they had arrived at the cabin from their wedding. They had gone for a walk and decided to pick some raspberries for a pie. The grave had been very near that of Clarke's infant daughter who had died the year before the war started. He had been married to Elizabeth then, she had never gotten over the little girl's death and had sent him a letter telling him she had filed for divorce while he had been away in the army. There was no marker at the sight of the new grave and some one had even scattered leaves from the surrounding woods to make it look less conspicuous. It was a half hearted attempt to disguise the grave site. Now that they thought of it in the present it was more like someone wanted to make the site itself look natural again than to hide the fact that it was ever there.

Seeing the Winslow's there again had upset Nancy much more than she had showed while the sheriff and all the other men were present.

They had decided one thing though, they would stay at Carr's house and farm the land rather than him take the job as superintendent of Twin Sugars Plantation. The discussions that had taken place between them convinced them both that they would rather work for themselves and try to build something of their own than work for some one else. The offer was deeply appreciated and they must tell Mabel soon of their decision. The trust she had shown by offering the position to them was very reassuring indeed. They hoped that Clarke may be able to work on the plantation during the slow periods of farming if he was needed and of course he would always be there for Mabel as a faithful neighbor if a need for either of them should arise again.

They had spoken to Carr to get his opinion about young Donald Persinger and his new bride Cassie being offered up for the superintendent's job. Carr had thought it an excellent idea, he said he thought the Persinger couple would be excellent for the McClung's. That night Donald and Cassie were coming to Clarke's for supper and the plan was they would approach them with the idea then. The job was not for Clarke to offer but if he could find out if they were interested then he could tell Mabel of his decision and offer Donald as a suitable alternative. He thought if Donald was agreeable to it he would also suggest Mason to be Donald' foreman, he would need a good man who had the trust of the former slaves who stayed on to work for Custus. That night he and Nancy did indeed broach the subject and the young couple was both thrilled with the idea of living in the big house and running the place for Mabel Morgan. Donald was also all for recommending Mason as the foreman. Clarke said he would plan on talking to the Morgan's on Thursday, two days away. Donald and Cassie stayed the night with them and the four stayed up late talking of their futures and plans for starting families and all four were optimistic about their futures now that the war and long trial were over.

The Winslow's went to find the sheriff the next afternoon and showed him the vest they had found at the sinkhole and again demanded that he arrest Clarke Lewis for murdering his brother. Sheriff Knight let out a long sigh and turned and looked at Basil. "I told you before we have no reason to arrest any one. First of all we do not know if Bill Winslow is even dead. Yes, I admit that finding his vest at that location does indicate that he probable is, but it does not prove it beyond a doubt. He could have lost his vest in the creek some how, or he could have fallen in to the creek, drowned and washed down in to the Seivey Hole. He could have decided that he was sick of you fellows and just moved on. He could be anywhere I don't damn know where he is and I am not going to arrest some one and charge them with murder when I do not even know if a murder has taken place. That Lewis boy that you want me to arrest was not even married when you say Bill was getting it on with his wife. His wife had never been in the Cold Knob region in her life until after the marriage. She could not have been the one Bill was seeing with her husband off in the war. The only thing unusual at all is the grave being on their property and it was empty when we opened it. Now I want you to listen to me Winslow, you have pushed the people in that valley as far as they are going to be pushed. You may have gotten off the murder charge with your money and influence, but don't think you can continue running rough shod over those people. Some one up there is going to kill you if you continue disrupting their lives. Now, get your ass out of my office and don't let me hear of you bothering any one else from that area again."

The brothers left in a huff telling Knight they knew they were wasting their time coming to him. That night and for the next three nights all they did was drink whiskey and talk of revenge on the citizens of Lewis Mill. Basil hardly slept at all during those three days, his mood only got darker as each hour passed. He seemed as obsessed with finding Bill as he had been that day of the shootings in the holler. There was no reasoning at all with him, he seemed convinced some one had killed Bill and if not because of love, then because of the love of money. He confided to Lawrence and Ross that some money had been missing that only Bill and himself had known about. Lawrence had over heard the conversation Basil had with Hudson their lawyer while they had been confined in the jail before the trial. He had never mentioned it to Ross and had been afraid to bring it up to Basil. Now that Basil had himself brought up the missing money, Lawrence tentatively suggested that perhaps Bill had just left with the money and his Rebel girl friend. This remark was answered with a backhand slap across his mouth that sent him to the floor of the tavern. He was told to never ever think that way about Bill, because the only way Bill had failed to come back was because he was dead.

He told Lawrence to get ready to ride. They were going back to Lewis Mill and this time someone was going to really pay for what they had done to their family. Ross said he could not go with them he was afraid his leg would start bleeding again if he got on a horse. Truth was, Ross had gone through tremendous pain on his last trip there and he had no intentions of ever going back toward Cold Knob again in his life. He never would have admitted this to Basil, of course, and his leg was still tender and barely healed. The two men who had accompanied Basil and Lawrence were sent for and informed of the plans and the four rode out just after daybreak on Sunday morning.

Basil was red eyed, unshaven and unkempt as they rode their fine horses toward Lewis Mill. Three days of alcohol and drunken assurances from each other, that mistreatment and disrespect were being visited on the Winslow family only fueled his desire for another confrontation with the people of the town. Each time a new bottle was opened they would talk out the last month's events, over and over, and it became clearer to them with each telling that they had indeed been terribly wronged. He uncorked another bottle from his fine leather saddlebags as they approached the village. He took a deep pull on the bottle and passed it to the others. They came to the log church with its two double doors and saw the horses, wagons and carriages parked outside. That it was the Sabbath

Day had never occurred to this band of Satan disciples and recognition of signs of assemblage to worship only served to heighten their desire to disrupt anything that represented normalcy and stability.

"Open the doors, Roland," barked Basil. "We're taking these horses to church."

Roland dismounted and threw open one side of the double doors and then the second one. Basil rode his horse right into the church and down the center isle toward the pulpit. The big bay stallion pranced on the pine floor, tossed his head from side to side and fought the reins in Basil's hand. All the women screamed and some men also, at the sudden interruption of services. Shock was on every face in the church including Reverend Rogers who was in the middle of his sermon titled Looking a Gift Horse in the Mouth. When he heard the noise and looked up from his notes the stallion was prancing not five feet away from the pulpit. In the saddle was a figure who looked like Lucifer himself, dressed in black and laughing hysterically, with blood red eyes and yellow teeth.

Shocked almost speechless the reverend started to speak, "See here man, See here." When he said that, Basil pulled his gun and shot three times in to the ceiling. The noise from the 44 caliber pistol, inside the building sounded like a cannon. The stallion jumped at the first shot and kicked out behind him knocking over the first row bench that landed with a bang nearly as loud as the pistol shot had made. Screams again were heard and Basil pulled the reins sharply turning the stallions head toward the front door. He spurred the stallion's sides and it carried him out the front door and off the small porch.

"That's for my two dead brothers, you pious shit heads!" he screamed as he galloped away from the church yard.

Lawrence, Roland and the other gang member who sat on their horses out side the church could not believe what Basil had just done. It took them a moment after he and his horse exited the church to regain their senses enough to follow him up the road.

He stopped about a mile up the road where it forked, the right went up to the Laurel Hill area and the left continued on up the mountain to Cold Knob. He had calmed somewhat from when he left the church but still seemed agitated. He was still on the edge, but not totally out of control as he had seemed to be when he had rode into the church. They didn't really know what to say to him and if they had the right words in their vocabularies they would not have dared express any opinion of his actions one way or the other. Lawrence had seen his brother's behavior deteriorate to the point of near insanity in the last month. Bill's disappearance and Sammie's death had affected him in some deep way that clouded his thinking to the point that any thing he did was not a surprise any more. Lawrence knew that what the sheriff said was true, if they kept pushing these people they would start to fight back irregardless of any threat of martial law and the sending of troops that the two judges had spoken of. He knew Basil would not tolerate any criticism from him in any way. He could only hope that Basil would decide they should leave this valley before he killed someone.

As the three calmer members of the Winslow party were resting their horses and hoping Basil would not explode in to another tirade before one of them got up the nerve to suggest they return to the Double Cross, Carl Blake was crossing the bridge just around the curve. They could not see him or he them until he would round the bend in the road and come up on the road crossing where they were sitting their horses. He was walking as was his general mode of transportation and he was headed to the village to have Sunday dinner with Margie Nimrod and whom ever she decided to invite from the church service she attended regularly down the road from her house. Carl lived with his mother Naomi, an elderly lady who sometimes would accompany him to Margie's but who on this Sunday begged off because her arthritis was acting up. Carl had taken to carrying his pistol with him whenever he left his home and the heavy Colt pulled on his light weight jacket and was a pain in the ass to lug around. The second beating he had endured from Basil Winslow had convinced him he needed some protection and despite the inconvenience he made a vowel to carry it. He was humming lightly to himself as he crossed the creek and looked at the cool rushing water under the bridge. When he rounded the turn, there in the road were four horses and riders and it took only a glance to see they were the riders that had make Carl become a pistol toting citizen.

In later years Carl would sometimes wonder if he, as he briefly wondered the last time he met these men, would have run or hid had he known they were there. He decided in those later years that he did not think he would have this last time. When Basil had beaten him the second time, he had made the decision as he lay in the dust, that he would have no more of this and he had told Basil the same after Carr had come out and threatened the men with his shot gun. When he saw the men in the road he knew that what he had warned them of was about to take place and he could no more stop what happened next than he could make the waters of Roaring Creek flow up stream. Still, he tried to walk past them with out an altercation. Roland was on the nearest side closest to Carl and he let him pass him without making any move or comment. Roland hoped that Basil would not beat this man again, he had witnessed the scene the week before and it was not a pretty sight.

"Hey," said Basil. "It's the expert witness. So, Mr. Witness, are you ready to get rope slapped again?"

As he spoke he removed his coiled rope from his saddle horn and slapped Carl across the face as before. The coiled rope immediately set his face to burning like fire and Basil laughed his crazy cackle laugh and swung the rope toward Carl again. This time he missed and his eyes opened in surprise and then narrowed just as quickly when he saw Carl pull the heavy Navy 44 caliber pistol out of his coat and point it up at him. He felt the impact of the heavy slug as it tore in to his chest and exploded his heart. Basil Winslow fell to his left side and hit the hard packed road with a thud. He was dead before the thud was heard however. Lawrence was next to see the open barrel of the 44 pointed right up at his chest. He threw up his empty hands and said "don't shoot, please don't shoot. The other two also let Carl know their hands were empty.

"I told him not to beat me again. He wouldn't listen, now, he's dead." Carl said calmly. "Now, I want you to each reach with your left hands, and throw your guns in to that field there."

He aimed the gun from one to the next as they threw away their side arms. Then, he made them throw the rifles from their scabbards in to the field.

"If any of you three or that other one that Custus shot, ever come back to this valley I promise you I will shoot you all. If I see you in Frankford or Lewisburg or any where else in this life I will just start shooting. I don't get out of this area much but some times I travel a little. So, if you don't want to die you need to clear out of Greenbrier County. Put his body back on that horse and get it out of here. I do not want that thing even buried in this county." Carl stood back and let them load Basil's remains back on his horse, they tied it across the saddle with the same rope he had three times beaten Carl Blake with.

The men each swore that they would leave the county that day and not come back. They said they were sorry for what trouble they had caused they people of the valley. Due to the circumstances, none of the three doubted in the least bit that Carl would make good on his promise if he saw them again. They went down the valley each vowing never to come back to this place. When they reached the church the crowd outside had swelled considerably. They saw the three upright riders and the one lying hogtied across the saddle approach with apprehension until they realized the cause of their misery this last month was never going to bother them again. The three living horsemen looked straight ahead and seemed not to know the crowd was even there. A cheer went up from some of the church group as the riders slowed to pass the crowd of buggies and farm wagons that lined the road by the church.

Cries of, "Don't come back here," and "that's sinkhole justice for you," were heard from the crowd as they continued on past the assemblage.

Carl carried the side arms and rifles he had taken from the gang and stacked them in the corner of the fence row. He then walked down to Margie's still hungry and still expecting they roast chicken and dumplings she was so well known for. When he reached her house he was surprised that no one was home. The reverend must be long winded today he thought. He looked down the road to the log church in the distance and saw a really large crowd of people on the outside. The thought crossed his mind that the remaining members of the gang had stopped there and were causing trouble. That did not seem to be realistic he decided after recalling the looks on their faces when they left him. He hiked down to the church and was told of Basil riding his horse into the church during services. He was also told that the riders had come back by there with Basil Winslow tied across his saddle and obviously dead. They were all joyous that the lord had provided justice for every one hurt in their town but some expressed concern for what could happen to Clarke Lewis when the new state government found out what he had done. They were all sure that Clarke had settled the score with Basil for killing Custus and burning Clarke's home on the creek.

Seeing that the wrong information could spread like wildfire, Carl went to the steps of the church and after asking and getting every one's attention. He told of what happened on the road earlier that day. He admitted with out remorse or regret that he was the one who had killed Basil Winslow, not Clarke and told of the beatings he had been forced to endure from Basil before. He had known nothing of the incident at the church that morning and said that the killing had nothing to do with revenge for anything Basil had done. It had been simply done because he refused to let Basil beat him again. He said that he did not think any of the Winslow gang would ever again cause them any problems. He planned to go to

Lewisburg after he had some of Margie's dumplings and turn himself in to the sheriff.

He did indeed have chicken and dumplings at Margie's before he left to find Sheriff Knight. Carr Lewis, Donald Persinger and John Morgan accompanied him to Lewisburg that afternoon. Morgan was to represent him legally and it was decided that Clarke should stay at home. Morgan advised that he stay behind and not give any one the chance to bring up his recent troubles with Basil.

CHAPTER 18

Self Defense Again?

They avoided the Frankford route and went out the Rader's Valley road and found the sheriff at his Lewisburg boarding house room. They told him the complete story and Morgan had an idea. He wanted his client arrested immediately and taking a page form the Winslow's trial he requested a trial by the sitting judge to take place the next day, Monday. The sheriff agreed and locked Carl up in the jail right then. The sheriff sent a deputy to the home of Judge Hailey requesting he come to his office right away. When the judge arrived he listened to what had taken place and was not at all surprised at the incident. He agreed to hear the case the next morning and suggested in lieu of the district attorney not prosecuting the case because of self defense it would be best to have a trial and find him innocent. That way the state could never come back and charge him again with murder at a later date. He would hear the case and make the decision and Carl could walk out a free man.

The next morning the case was called, heard and Carl was found innocent by reason of self defense. He was allowed to go free. Morgan advised him to go somewhere else for a time just to be sure the state would not come up with some other trumped up charge. John and Mabel had a cabin on the Maury River at Goshen Pass and offered it to Carl for a while. He gave him directions to the site and told him he would be notified when it was safe to return to Lewis Mill. Carl was also given the name of a man who lived nearby the cabin who would see he had everything he needed. Carl's mother Naomi would be cared for at Twin Sugars until he could return. He said his mother would, he was sure, prefer to spend the time with Margie Nimrod. They had been friends for years and he knew that would be what they would both prefer. He was very thankful for all Morgan had done for him.

The whole case was finished and all the details worked out by noon. Carl caught a ride with a freight hauler from Big Clear Creek named Elmore Dalton who was taking a load of lumber to Lexington. The other three, Carr, Morgan and Persinger were back at Lewis Mill by seven o'clock that night. They passed through Frankford and paused to look at the Double Cross. Some one had turned the sign over and nearly scratched away Audrey's and written in a childish scrawl,

> ABBY AND NORA'S
> FOOD, DRINK AND
> CARING COMPANIONSHIP
> NEW CLIENT'S WELCOME

Chapter 19

Peace at Last

Life was peaceful in the village and surrounding hills for the next number of years. Mabel and John Morgan turned the running of the plantation over to Donald and Cassie Persinger after Clarke rejected their offer and moved their family back to Covington that fall. The Persinger's lived out their lives in the grand house on the mountain and raised three sons there enjoying the magnificent view every day of their lives. Mason McClung stayed on as foreman and also raised a family there. He and his wife built a Cape Cod style house on the road to Cold Knob just beneath the jutting peak that bordered it. Their off spring and the Persinger children and all of the children of the mountain plantation found, when they became adults, the extreme climate was too harsh for them and they ended up in the large cities of the north. The neglected houses suffered from the effects of abandonment and though it took until well into the next century the fields turned back into forest.

Carr married Melinda and they did just what Rufus Brown had envisioned when he left his business to Carr. They took care of the neighbors and kept the thriving business vibrant with the introduction of new ideas that were mostly from

Melinda's sharp business mind. Carr acquired property all up both sides of Roaring Creek and on the east side of Cherry Hill. Clarke and Nancy never rebuilt in the holler. The larger house accommodated their four children better and they lived there until they passed away after their children were grown to adulthood. Upon his death Carr willed the seventy acre farm and house to Clarke and Nancy. One of their daughters and her husband rebuilt on the original house site in the holler and they raised a large family there. While not rich by any means the farm kept their needs met and supplied them with a living.

Both the Lewis brothers were able to put the war behind them and never burdened their family or friends with reminders of the terrible ordeal they had endured.

Carl Blake returned to the area after a few months had passed. Nothing was ever heard from any other authorities concerning the shooting. He lived out his life there and rarely mentioned the incident that Sunday morning that, though extremely out of character for him, had brought a peace and finality to the ordeal wrought by Basil Winslow and his brothers. He carried a pistol every day of his life after the incident with the Winslows although he did trade the heavy Navy 44 for a much lighter weapon.

Sidney Sammons never got locked up again and attended church twice a week until he died seventeen years after he had been in the same jail with Basil and Lawrence Winslow. He and Reverend Rogers always insisted that Bill Winslow had gone down the Sievey Hole at the sinks of the creek and that the community was a better place because of it.

Reverend Rogers always felt that the hand of the Lord must have been guiding the incidents that took place after Basil rode his stallion into the house of God while service was being conducted. He, in later years would on occasion use the incident in one of his sermons specifically that God is not mocked. He always felt that Basil had attempted to defile the house of God and that Carl was used as God's instrument in striking the blow against blasphemy. He had coined the phrase concerning the missing Bill Winslow, that what happened to all of the brothers was just a case of sinkhole justice.

Bill Winslow's disappearance was never solved. He became a thing of legend and for year's parents would threaten their children to be good, or, Bill Winslow will get you. Any strange or mysterious happening that occurred was always said to be Bill Winslow trying to find his way back to his brothers. Eventually his disappearance and the misery and strife it caused was remembered by only the oldest in the community and then by no one still alive. Some of the younger residents had heard something about a man missing a long time ago but never knew the details.

Eight years after the grave in the holler was opened and found empty, Carr and Melinda were on a buying trip to Danville on the Virginia/North Carolina border. They were examining bolts of cloth in a mill store there on the river when he saw a familiar looking face behind the counter. It turned out to be his second cousin Theo Lewis who he had not seen in nearly twenty years. Theo and his family had left Greenbrier when the boys were only about ten years old. Carr could recall only seeing him once since, that had been at a family reunion on Culbertson Creek years ago. Carr's grandfather Hezekiah Lewis and Theo's grandfather Horace were brothers. They had both been born and brought up in a log cabin in the holler that had long since gone back to nature. Hezekiah had shown his grandson Carr the cabins location long ago. It was just above the knoll that held the two graves and the only thing still there was four rocks that had been used for the foundation. In the spring, daffodils, offspring of originals planted years ago when his grandfather had been a boy marked the spot in bright yellow blooms.

Theo said Horace never liked the Danville area and spent his days pining for the broad savannahs of Greenbrier and his deceased wife who was buried near the mill two years to the day after the couple moved with their son, Theo's dad and his family to the mill town. He said Grand Pop did finally come out of his doldrums enough to convince them he could manage on his own and he returned to the Greenbrier area.

He spent his last years unbeknown to the Danville Lewis's living at the Poor Farm on the Williamsburg/Frankford road. He must have had someone there help him with correspondence because he wrote the family regularly in the last years of his life. They thought he was living in Williamsburg at the hotel there and were shocked to receive a letter from a Mr. Bobbitt at the Poor Farm that he had lived there for four years and had passed away. He died in April and left instructions for the burial to take place at the site of his birth on Roaring Creek.

Mr. Bobbitt said they had complied with his wishes and buried him at the requested place just above a deserted cabin. When the family, who had done quite well in the textile business received the news they were determined to bring Grand Pop back to rest beside his beloved wife near them in Danville. They contacted a funeral establishment and had the body disinterred and brought back to them for burial. Horace now lay beside his other love in life besides the holler, his faithful wife Ivy.

Since the cabin near the grave was deserted, Theo and his family assumed that Hezekiah's family had moved away or been killed in the war. This was the response to Carr's inquiry as to why none of them had been told of the burial.

This chance encounter with a long lost relative solved the eight year old mystery of the empty grave. A mystery that caused so much heart ache and misery for a small mountain village that had already had suffered through the terrible war.

Chapter 20

A Right Smart Boy

The old man sat under the swaying palm trees and watched the surf pound the white sand beach. Sea gulls flew back and forth scolding one another and arguing over any piece of debris that the current may bring ashore. The large white southern style planter's house sat back in the trees behind his beach front gazebo. He spent most of the days now at the gazebo gazing out at the beautiful emerald waters that surrounded the house on three sides. Sometimes, one or all of his three female companions would spend time with him under the palms. He would watch his grand children play in the sand, building castles and moats filled with sea water that they said protected them from their enemies.

He did little work at all now and no physical labor. The running of his rubber tree business he had long since turned over to his oldest son. His days were now spent enjoying the outdoors and shade trees. He cared little for the sun's heat and the cool aqua water, he just stayed in the shade now. The only exception was when he went out past the breakers for the flounder and conch that make up most of their diet. His hair that had one time been a sandy color was now mostly white and the beard he wore closely clipped was all white. He was of medium height and weight that had changed little over the forty odd years he had lived in the Caicos Islands.

He had first landed in Nassau in the Bahamas where he lived for a year. He had been there just a short time when he noticed a lot of Americans coming to the island. He did not want to be recognized, so when the opportunity to move to Middle Caicos Island came up he moved there and bought a run down rubber plantation that was being sacrificed by a family of Tories who wished to return to England. They were the third generation of loyal British who had been run out of New Jersey when Cornwallis surrendered his forces at Yorktown. They had lost most of their money and all of their property because of their loyalties to the crown and ended up on this island trying to eek out a living for seventy years.

The plantation was bought just as he found it, furniture and all. The family had a young Irish house maid who showed a reluctance to return to the old country. She stayed with him and though they never married they produced a boy and a girl from the doing of the thing as he liked to call it. Over the years he added two more doers, both young brown skinned beauties who produced three more children that grew up and produced children of their own that he now watched play in the sun. His off springs, off spring were as varied in color as a vest he once saw and he loved each one equally.

Sometimes when he was on the beach his mind would wander back to the circumstances that brought him to this paradise. He would close his eyes and listen to the pounding surf and the laughter of the playing children and think back to that day in May, 1865.

The soldier, the wolf, and the mule made the two mile trek to the secluded shack that he had left behind in the cove below Grassy Knob. Morgan was anxious to get home and the thought of seeing Maggie and laying with her again in their rope bed awoke an arousal in him. He had not been with a woman since he joined the army over two years ago and though he had not missed his wife in any deep caring way, the physical part had him looking forward to their reunion. He dismounted and tied the mule and the wolf to separate grubby trees in the dirt yard that served as a lawn for the little clapboard house with the small front porch with a swing on one side. He mounted the steps and was met by red haired, freckled Maggie who heard the footsteps on the porch. The smile on her face faded quickly when she saw it was him. She had obviously expected someone else to be standing on the porch.

"Oh" she said, It's you, I thought you were dead."

"It's pretty obvious, you were expecting some one else." He stated.

She stood there looking at him like he was a ghost. She started to say something but stammered briefly and then though better of it. He reached for her and hugged her to him, she stiffened and shied away like he smelled bad. He realized that he probably did smell bad but he had stopped and bathed as best he could in a couple of streams on the trip home. He had not had a bath before that since the previous fall, just before he left the army. He did not think that her aloofness was due just to his lack of proper hygene though, something was up, and he needed to find out what. He walked past her into the living room and noticed the smell of apple pie coming from the kitchen. She must have known he was coming after all, he wryly thought. She was very nervous as he walked to the stove and cut a piece of the pie for himself and poured a cup of coffee. As he ate the pie, she kept saying over and over. I thought you were dead, I thought you were dead. He savored the sweetness of the pie and returned for another piece. She finally told him that he could not stay there and he answered that of course he could stay there, this was his house. He was home from the war and ready to start their life over in marital bliss.

She told him, after he asked her several times what was wrong, that she had someone else and that he had to leave before that someone came back. She told him if he did not leave he would be killed. She had taken up with a man who had a vicious temper and notorious reputation. He and his brothers were known as a rough crowd and he used a gun to settle arguments like a lawyer used a courtroom and a boxer used his fists.

"Why did you take up with a man like that?" he asked.

"I was by myself and I though you were dead and never coming back. He rode here one day looking for land to buy and we got to talking. He found out I was by myself and he started coming by to help me and one thing lead to another. He's not mean with me, he's gentle. I think he cares for me like you never did. He touches something in me that you never could. I want you to leave here and never come back. All you and I ever had was that other thing anyway. So just leave"

Morgan looked at her, letting all this settle in. If he just left now he would be giving up his little house and not much else. He knew that he could easily find someone to give him more of them selves than Maggie ever had. Maybe I will just take the wolf and mule and mosey on out of here.

Just then the wolf began snarling in the yard and the sound of hooves on the hard packed soil of the lane could be heard.

"Leave now, go out the back door and run," she hissed.

"I will not run from my own place," said Morgan.

The front door opened and the man who walked in could have been Morgan's brother, they were the same height, build and even had the same color hair and eyes. This man however, had a mean hard look to him and walked like he had seen a lot of trouble in his life and was looking for more.

"Who are you and what do you want here." He said in a low and menacing tone of voice.

"This is my house and I 'm home from the war. I know what you want here but I don't know who you are. My name is Morgan Eggleston now, what is your name?"

"My name is Bill Winslow. There's nothing here for you now, so take your hound and mule and hit the road. I'm taking your wife your house and your garden. Don't ever come back here, you stinking piece of shit Reb."

Something snapped inside Morgan. A red haze seemed to almost blind him. He thrust his jaw forward and said evenly.

"All of that huh, and I just walked three weeks to f--k my wife." He seemed to know this would set Winslow off and it did. He dug for his gun and fired at Morgan from across the room. The shot just missed his head and went through the propped open window above the wood box. His second shot hit Maggie in the throat as she ran toward him shouting,

"No, don't shoot."

Monroe threw a heavy iron he grabbed from the sideboard and hit Winslow just as he squeezed the trigger. The top of the iron struck him between the eyes and the bottom of it flattened his nose in to his cheeks in a gush of blood. The whole thing happened in like two minutes from the time Winslow walked in the front door. Monroe crossed the room to look at Maggie, she was already dead in a pool of blood. Her green eyes were staring straight ahead as she lay on the kitchen floor. She seemed to be looking straight at him as if she was saying, why did you have to come home? Winslow eyes were gone, they had disappeared somewhere back in his head behind the irons handle. The iron was stuck in his face handle first but the handle was crossways, horizontal and looked kind of bizarre, like it was attached the wrong way. How can an iron protruding from some ones face ever be considered the wrong way, he thought.

Morgan smelled something burning and moved the apple pie to the back of the stove. He sat down on one of the kitchen chairs and held his head in his hands. How did this happen? He asked himself. Less than an hour ago he had eagerly trotted the mule up the lane, excited about returning home. Now his wife was dead and her lover too, in the blink of an eye. He looked through his fingers at Winslow and regretted baiting him. "I could hang for this", he said out loud. He allowed himself to slowly calm down and his heart stopped hammering in his chest. He had killed Winslow in self defense the man had been shooting at him for Christ's sakes. Maggie had been shot by Winslow accidently. He had nothing to do with that. Be reasonable, he thought, how would some one on the outside look at this? A soldier comes home from the war after being gone over two years and finds his wife with another man. He kills them both. That's just the way this will be perceived by everyone, including a judge. They will not believe that the boyfriend killed the wife and certainly not that the husband killed the boyfriend in self defense.

You'll think of something, you're a right smart boy, his grandfather used to say to him as a child. His mind raced and nothing came to him that could be a solution to this mess he was in. He had spent the last six months in a jail cell. He did not want to go back for something he was not guilty of and the gallows would be a real possibility he knew. Just then the wolf began howling, it was a distraction at first but then he started to think of the different scenarios. The solution came to him all at once and he began setting the staged scene. Morgan began removing Winslow's clothes, even his underwear. When he had the body completely naked he stripped off his raggedy clothing and placed them on the corpse. He then dressed himself in Winslow's expensive duds and was surprised that even the boots fit. He carried Winslow's body through the living room and down the porch steps and laid it down on the ground.

He carefully stretched Maggie's body out with out disturbing the angle of her head. The bullet had exited her neck after it tore through her throat and must have gone out of the room through the open window. He checked the wall carefully and could find no sign anywhere that the spent bullet struck any thing in the kitchen. He then took the belt and knife with scabbard that he had worn home and slipped the belt around Winslow's waist. He removed the thin wedding band he had worn for six years and slipped it on the left hand ring finger of the corpse.

Now it was time for the hard part, he sat a moment and thought about what he had to do. After a few minutes of playing it out in his mind he arose and with a deliberate pace he went out and untied Wolf. He removed the heavy leather muzzle and rope and holding him by the collar he guided him past Winslow's body and up the front porch steps and into the kitchen. Morgan had heard Sharlot brag about and describe Wolf's attacks on the prisoners and slaves. He said that when he wanted someone to be taken by the throat or face he would tell Wolf to "Bring blood, Bring blood." Morgan fought back bile in his throat when he gave Wolf the signal to tear out his wife' throat from her dead body. The taste of blood seemed to spur him on in a frenzy of gnashing teeth. Morgan fought back screams of revulsion as all evidence of the bullets entrance and exit was eliminated. Even the most thorough of medical exams would reveal no evidence of the guns use.

He pulled the wolf out of the kitchen with all of his strength and hurried him down the steps to the body of Winslow. Morgan was afraid if he stopped for even a second he would not be able to continue this vile but necessary act. He positioned himself where he could slip the knife in to Wolf's heart exactly where it would enter had he himself been on the ground and was being eaten alive by this blood crazed beast. He took a deep breath and gave Wolf the signal to attack. He ripped and tore in to the already mutilated face of Winslow, and there was soon no part of the man's head or neck above the torso that was recognizable at all. Morgan plunged the knife up in to the wolf's chest to the hilt. He turned and looked at Morgan for a second with blood and tissue in his teeth and made a last effort to bite him before he shuddered and took his last breath. Morgan pulled the iron out of what was left of the corpse's face and tossed it in to some tall weeds near the well He sat on the steps for a few minutes catching his breath before he went inside and looked through the drawers and all the hiding places for anything that might belong to Winslow. He had been spending some time there and Morgan found two changes of clothing and a rain coat in the bedroom. Under the bed, he also found a black valise with a hidden side pocket, inside was twenty eight thousand dollars in U.S. notes. Gathering everything he tied it all together in a bed roll, he also took some ham and biscuits from the cupboard. The last thing he did was untie the mule and put him in the small field back of the house, he went straight to the heavy clover on the back side of the field.

Morgan surveyed the scene in the yard and mounted the black gelding, then he dismounted ran up the porch steps and propped open the front door. The wolf would not have able to open the front door to get to Maggie. He stood on the porch and ran through everything in his mind. Had he forgotten anything else? He made one more pass through the house and even stepped out the back door to the small rear stoop. He saw something hanging on the post by the gate to the garden. Two new boards stood out in the gate as if someone had just recently repaired it. It was a leather vest made of varying shades of brown leather ranging from light to dark sections. Winslow must have been repairing the gate and got hot and removed it in the heat. Morgan grabbed the vest and walked to the edge of Roaring Creek and tossed it in to the rushing brown water. It had rained recently in the mountains because the creek was swollen and high. The vest was swept away down stream in an instant.

Satisfied that he had covered everything he rode out just after dark and took the Cold Knob Road over the mountain to Richwood. The next morning found him in the best hotel there registered under the name of Patrick Long. After sleeping most of the day he took a long bath and ate a steak. The next morning he was on the road to Baltimore where he planned to catch a steamer to Nassau in the Bahamas. This was where the white beaches and emerald water he had dreamed about were. In the hotel lobby he found a copy of the Pocahontas Times with sketches of paradise and he decided this would be his destination.

One week later, he was wearing a white tropical suit and hat, as he walked down the gang plank to board the sleek steamer in Baltimore harbor. His grandfather's words came to mind,

"You're a right smart boy, Morg, you're think of something."

THE END

About the Author

Emerson "Willie" Williams was born and raised in Trout, WV. and still maintains a home in Greenbrier County. He is a resident of Goochland County, Va. and is an avid amateur Civil War historian. His first novel was Roaring Creek, about his g' great grand father and his brothers experiences in the Confederate army. Sinkhole Justice begins with their return home at the wars end as they begin rebuilding their lives. It can be enjoyed as a sequel to Roaring Creek or as a stand alone novel. Correspondence is welcomed at emersonwms@yahoo.com

Printed in the United States
201587BV00002B/1-168/A

9 781434 340689